DELIRIUM WILDERNESS

CRAIG A. BROCKMAN

CONTENTS

Prologue

I awoke in the Delirium Wilderness; the Native kid looked as if he were dead. I could not remember his name—or mine. A blood smear trailed down the round fender of a rusty pickup truck and ended above his head. He lay twisted, his arm carelessly draped on the running board, his small hand gray and helpless.

Slate clouds roiled overhead, lowering until the pointed teeth of balsam and black spruce pierced the dark canopy. Leaves and debris were lifted by zephyrs from other worlds and skittered like tiny feet across the clearing until they tumbled over the hulk of the old truck and whirled into the black forest again.

"Duane," I said hoarsely, remembering his name. I coughed, my head pulsing like the school fire alarm gnawing at my brain. I would not accept that he was dead. "Duane, we have to..." My tongue too heavy to speak. The clouds pressed near, surrounding us in darkness.

I tried to hold onto consciousness, sensing a looming danger in the swamp nearby. Something lurked darker and more deadly than the storm, watching us, ready to pounce.

From around the scabby tree trunks, I heard guttural cackling.

Wavering from the deep huffing of an ape to the high whining of a hyena, a swinish creature mocked, trying to regurgitate words.

I shifted, trying to see Duane more clearly. Was he sobbing? The voice imitated a child's cries. Then another of the horrid voices chimed in as they closed around the clearing, howling and echoing the gibberish of each other.

The darkening skies closed over me, and my consciousness faded again.

1

THE FAIRY IN THE BERRY CAN

"STAY AWAY FROM THERE, Scotty. If Dee's drunk, ya never know if some bull in a rut is shackin' up with her over there, again," Grandma called, standing on the porch, her fists thrust in her waist, elbows flaring. My two favorite remembrances of her are either wearing that stained apron with the little pink and blue flowers or sitting by the Christmas tree with a glass of brandy, a slice of fruit cake balanced on her knee, and a big grin.

"I'm just going to see if Duane's around, then I'm riding into town," I answered.

"Get back before supper 'case I need help with that damn sink in Cabin 3," she said, "And watch out on the highway."

She was not a mean grandma. Quite the opposite. It's only that she did not throttle her tongue and her engine had no setting for idle. I try to sweep away images of her last years when she would shuffle, oxygen strapped to her walker, smoking her Camels and tending the cabins.

Duane was Dee's kid: smart and bust-a-gut funny for his age. According to Grandma they'd landed here from a Menominee reservation in Wisconsin. I didn't care where they came from, I only knew that there were no other kids around and we always figured out some silly way to have fun despite our age difference. I was older, but not old enough to understand the silent torment that he endured while living with a mother who spent her days in a fog of alcohol and weed, while entertaining a cavalcade of crude and abusive men.

She would yell at Duane whenever he called her *Ma*: too damn young for some kid's Ma. Probably true. So he had always called her Dee.

Grandma's place was called Shirley's Cabins and it stood along the shimmering shores of Lake Superior just a couple of miles south of Paradise in Michigan's Upper Peninsula. It seemed as though I had spent every summer of a divine childhood there. However, knowing how memory works, it was probably only a couple of years and only a few weeks each year helping with cabins, then fishing or tearing around on my bike. And my childhood was not divine. Sometimes Grandma's place only made it seem that way.

There was a dock lined with bobbing rowboats, a small horseshoe of beach, and six clean, yellow cabins with imitation log siding. In the woods north of Grandma's house stood three cabins that were split from the plot before my grandparents bought it. In the sixties those three cabins were stranded along a sandy driveway that curved back around to the highway amid scrubby pines, berry bushes, and trash. The largest of the three had been maintained as a shoddy year-round rental and the other two were used as sheds to store junk. Duane and Dee lived in the ramshackle larger cabin.

I pumped my bike around the bend, weaving in the soft dirt, and hopped off in front of the cabin. Behind Dee's old Ford sedan stood a beat-up red pickup. At the top of a few broken-down steps the front door was wide open, even though the mosquitoes back here could flay flesh and the deer flies circled nearby with fork and knife ready to finish off the scraps.

Before my foot creaked on the first step, I heard a man's voice from inside the dim cabin mumbling a string of curses followed by, "Hey girl, we gonna smoke this thing?"

Out of the darkness Dee emerged giggling and slurring. Older-looking and more haggard than the last time I saw her, wearing only a thin tank top and a pair of short denim cut-offs, her vacant eyes downcast. "Duane went out back by the berry patch. Go on," she said flicking back her long, black hair and slamming the door.

At my age I knew four types of females: First there were family, which speaks for itself, then there were girls-who-might-talk-to-me—which were few, next there were outta-my-league, which included all high school girls and especially the cheerleaders, then finally there were women. Dee was a woman, though she was not much taller than me and she was probably only a couple of years ahead of my older brother, Seth. Despite my limited experience, I was pre-adolescent enough to notice this young woman. She was definitely a woman, and besides, she was somebody's mother.

I circled past car parts, an old toilet, rotting lumber, and all the other debris that had been scattered among pine trees and birches, until I found the path leading to the beach. The path split left toward the blackberry patch that lay in a clearing about as wide as a kid could throw a stone. That's why we came back here to play. It was far away, we could throw stuff, and it was the only open area near Duane's house where we could shoot my BB gun.

Across the middle of the clearing, like a great snow drift, the berry patch grew with canes of white blossoms reaching twice as high as Grandma. By late summer the branches would bow with fat berries that were prized by the few neighbors nearby, especially those lumbering, surly neighbors that lived in the woods—the black bears—desperate to fatten up for their winter nap.

"Duane?" I called. He didn't answer so I skirted to the other side of the patch. "Hey, Duane!"

"Back here," I heard from inside the mound of tangled thorns. "Find the tunnel."

Curious, I walked a few steps further, bent at the waist, until I saw the small arch that receded under the white ceiling of flowers. At the end of the tunnel, far in the middle of the berry patch, I saw Duane kneeling in a clearing no bigger than a camp tent. Duane's fine, black hair usually stuck out like a bunch of marsh grass, making him look like a surprised porcupine, but Dee had given him his summer buzz so now he was uniformly fuzzy.

He beckoned me with a finger. "C'mon." His face was sullen and unreadable. He did not flash his usual big smile. And he did not let loose with the usual tirade of chatter that would include two or three eager plans for our adventures. He was quiet.

Before I reached the end of the tunnel, he laid onto his stomach, looking pensively into the tiny room canopied with blossoms. I crawled up beside him and noticed the dried gulches of silent sadness that traced his dirty cheeks. I was twelve. I didn't know the words to say, or how to manage the brief awkward silence.

"What are you doing?" I blurted. Of course, I knew he was probably hiding, but I wanted to change the subject.

"Look." His face brightened immeasurably into a crooked grin. "It's under here."

He pointed with a stick toward an old, blue porcelain camp kettle, overturned and partly buried, dappled with moss. He slowly edged the end of the stick forward until I grabbed his arm. I imagined anything from a nest of hornets to a badger living under there. He looked at me, shook his head, and made a wan smile. I slowly let go. Resting the stick on the top of the pot, he carefully pushed. The stick slid off the slick surface, I flinched, and the kettle fell back. He tried again. This time the kettle tilted. At first I saw nothing, only darkness and gray sand.

"See? There she is," he said.

I cautiously scuttled a little closer but still saw only darkness.

"Back there. It's Rosy." His smile broadened. "Rosy the Fairy."

Because of Duane's colorful imagination we had played some strange games together. So I never knew what to expect. He tipped the pot further back, and there it was. Delicate and mysterious as a Luna moth, a small, white figure stood as though newly unfurled only for two boys to admire.

My older, jaded brain soon realized that it was no more than an errant weed or blackberry shoot that had produced a fan of white leaves while it struggled to grow under the darkness of the old kettle. But I loyally played along.

"Hi Rosy, posey, how's it hangin'?" I said.

"No, dummy. You have to ask her for a wish. One wish a day, that's all ya get."

"Oh, that's how it works. So, what did you ask her for?" I said, looking at him with a goofy grin.

Looking serious, he pursed his lips, looked down, and quickly shook his head. I should have known better than to ask.

"Ok, I'll ask for a wish, or did you use them all up already?"

Brightening, he shook his head once quickly while pushing the top of the kettle further back, bringing the stunted plant in full view. "Go ahead. Ask her!"

"Um...let's see. I wish, I wish that Duane's farts didn't stink so bad."

"No. A real wish." He laughed.

I rested my chin on my hands, peering at the sad little sprout, and made a wish. I hoped that two boys asking for the same wish did not cancel each other out.

On the way back, he tapped a stick on the trail and smacked trees and said matter-of-factly, "I'm gonna see if Dee wants to ask Rosy for a wish."

"Are you sure? I mean, do you think she's going to want to crawl all the way back there?" Knowing that he was probably in for a severe disappointment.

He looked away, unconcerned.

"Um," I stopped. I was stalling for time. "So, why did you name her Rosy? It doesn't sound much like a Fairy's name. Shouldn't it be like Tinkerbell or Dingleberry or something?"

"It's Ma...I mean Dee's name: Rose Delight White Bird," He stared at me confused for an instant as though I should have known, as though her name were obvious to everyone. Then he meandered ahead to the cabin.

Dee was milling around behind the house looking dazed, smoking a cigarette, and humming to herself. The red pickup gone, she had pulled on a long-sleeved shirt and shabby sweatpants. Seeing us, she folded her arms, smiling crookedly.

"So, where you boys been?" she asked in a weird giddy tone.

"The berry patch. Wanna see?" Duane said hopefully.

"What's in the berry patch? A little early for berries, ain't it?" she said, weaving as she tried to focus on her son.

I was silent, waiting for the mortification.

"The berries are all blossoms and there's a surprise." Duane smiled.

She shrugged and waved her hand. "Let's go."

I was worried as I trailed behind, Duane waving his stick and Dee shuffling along distracted.

It took more than a little coaxing to get her to crawl into the tunnel, though she was soon impressed as any mother with the array of white blossoms arching above her.

I told them that I would hang back by the woods to watch for bears, sensing this was a private moment for Duane, or maybe I just wanted to avoid the scene.

Before I'd taken a few steps, I heard Dee inside the berry patch. "There's my berry can. Well, dammit, Duane why didn't you just bring it home? I had to drag my ass all the way back here just to get an old kettle?"

A metallic thunk preceded a wail from Duane.

"Well get your damn big head out of the way. The kettle was stuck, and it just came loose. Jeez, sorry!" she scolded.

Soon Dee scuttled out of the berry patch, kettle in hand, and stumbled back to the cabin.

I leaned over to crawl into the tunnel, but Duane was already scrambling out, crying, his hand covering his eye. He pushed past me, heading for the beach while leaving me standing stupidly.

I wandered back to get my bike, skirting the junk around the cabin. Thankfully Dee was nowhere.

Later in the afternoon, I returned from town. Out of curiosity, I turned down the sandy road past the old cabins. As I came closer, I slowed. Dee sat on the broken front steps, face downturned, washed hair framing the cleaned and polished blue kettle. Her hands spread on each side as she looked helplessly into the depths of the empty Fairy can. Sad and broken, she looked up at me. Using pursed lips, she pointed toward the cabin and nodded a tiny salute as I rode past. I did not want to see Duane or endure another scene. I shook my head quickly and rode to Grandma's.

A week later the cabin was locked up and *Dee and the kid* had left according to Grandma.

I spent much of the summer with Grandma until I had to reluctantly go home for a couple of weeks to have my dreaded sports physical, a haircut, and an even more dreaded dentist appointment. When I got back, I figured that Duane's cabin would still be empty and I didn't know if I would ever see my friend again.

I was back at Grandma's cabins, and I was determined to make this final week of summer matter. It was getting on in August, nearing that time when every kid wakes up in the morning gasping for air amid nightmares of getting up for school, being late for the bus, or blowing pea soup through your nose when laughing in the cafeteria.

Grandma hardly had time to say *hell-o* before I hopped on my bike, spinning my tire while steering for town along the sandy driveway that seemed lonely without Duane. My head was down while navigating ruts, looking for the hard pack dirt.

"Hey, champ!" I nearly toppled, startled by a friendly voice as I passed the old cabin. A man with a gray ponytail and blue shirt stood on the neat, new landing that had been added to the cabin. He held a hammer in one hand and a carpenter's level in the other. A shiny black Chevy pickup was parked along the short two track next to the cabin.

I slid to a stop.

"Are you Scotty?" he said.

"Uh, yeah." I said, wary that he knew my name. I had seen too many strange men lurking around Dee's cabin.

"Duane told me all about you. Your little friend in need..." He waved me toward the cabin.

I laid down my bike and cautiously stepped forward. But before I could make it to the cabin, Duane came skipping around the corner. His hair was once more in full, black bristle from a summer's growth.

"Scotty!" He dropped his stick and ran to me. "Pop, this is Scotty."

The whole place had been spruced up almost like a real house and much of the junk had been hauled away.

Duane beckoned me around back with a conspiratorially curled finger and a big smile.

In the shade of a tall white pine a card table had been set up, strewn with empty pans and other utensils. In the center of the table stood that blue porcelain kettle, brimming with glistening blackberries.

"Hey. Scotty, our boy." I turned to see Dee coming from the cabin. Radiant. Her engaging brown eyes nearly made me blush, looking very much like one of those outta-my-league girls. Her hair was a little shorter but shiny and full, she wore a pink tee shirt, black jeans, and stepped smartly over to us in new brown sandals.

Her appearance rendered me speechless—for so many reasons.

"Yeah, Ma. Scotty, our boy. Our little boy. So cute, eh?" Duane mocked.

I punched him on the shoulder.

"Hey, why don't you guys get me another pan of berries so I can top off this batch," she said, waving us on with a cake pan.

It was fun to hear his chatter again as we tripped down the path. I had missed him.

"I like your grandpa," I said.

"Yeah, I know, Pop is fixing up the cabin while Ma's in school." A rotten stick exploded as he whacked it against a tree trunk. "I stayed with him while she was in the hospital." He paused, smiling at me. "That's when Rosy helped us."

"What do you mean?"

Picking up another dry stick he looked at me incredulously. "Rosy the Fairy, crazy head. I made a wish. Remember? Then Rosy got freed from the berry can. She couldn't answer my wishes when she was stuck in the dark under that old kettle." He clawed a wrinkled puff ball from the side of the trail. "You have to uncover them fairies so they can see the light and be free. That's how Ma was saved." He pitched the dry fungus in the air and hit it like a slugger. It exploded in a brown cloud, and he pumped his fist.

The north edge of the blackberry patch had been torn and crushed by those bumbling forest neighbors, scooping paws full of berries while resting on their broad haunches during their clumsy feast. But the tunnel had been undisturbed as Duane led me under swaying canes amid a fragrance of sweet, fermenting berries that squished under our knees and stained our hands. Arriving at the center, he hurriedly waved me forward. I plodded forward trying to avoid thorns and berries.

"Look, Scotty. She's here. She's all free now."

I approached with a puzzled look, prepared to oblige his hungry imagination once more.

There she stood. In the bronze light of a late summer afternoon, born from the bruised imagination of one hopeful child, an apparition proudly unfurled. Clothed in pink blossoms, with moss green leaves stood a proud wild rose with fragrance that surpassed the wine-scented berries.

Duane beamed a smile that is burned in my memory.

The fairy under the berry can, that had dwelt in darkness, was free.

2

Bound Road

BY CONTRAST DUANE WOULD have thought my home on Bound Road was idyllic. But it was not that simple.

"We're glory bound for snow bound," my dad said more than once before a big lake-effect snow. Watching those shear mile-high walls of dusky white cloud tilting toward us from Lake Superior was electrifying. It could mean snow days from school or just the thrill of head-high drifts and snow tunnels deep, cool and frosted with our breath.

But the origin of Bound Road was not glory bound or snow bound. It was artless as Mr. Bound. He was a lumberman who cut a lot of trees in the region in a century long gone. But the trees won. Our forty acres bristled with pickets of tall white pine and stickle-back ridges of hemlock and spruce.

Bound road was a straight shot south to north ending not far from the shores of Brimley Bay on the east end of Lake Superior. The lake-effect storms blew out of the northwest and crossed Bound Road at just the right angle to cover open areas in fender-deep drifts for days. The county plows only created taller snowbanks that trailed deeper drifts. Then the county would release Jurassic snow throwing trucks with rows of churning augers that devoured huge drifts and flung rainbow-tall arcs far afield.

Hidden from the road by a row of spruce, our ranch house stood covered in board and batten cedar, grayed with age. Birch and pine scattered across the yard and ran down to a creek that snaked through the middle of our forty.

Dad worked as a scheduler. I never understood what he did. He worked at Lake Superior State University, and my young imagination envisioned him scheduling everything from classes and hockey games to when the toilet paper was changed in the bathroom stalls. But I don't think that was his job.

Mom was a church secretary, so she did everything that was important at church.

Seth, strong and quiet, was a good brother. I often wondered if he had many friends. I believe he liked people, was always affable and funny, but I don't believe he *needed* people and was just as happy reading and hunting as he was hanging out after school with the guys.

I was like him, I suppose. I spent half my summer away from people, except when I was hanging out with my young pal, Duane.

My little sister Peety had Down syndrome. Her nickname was derived from Petra, a name given to make her strong—and, I suppose it was a play on the black dirt she mashed into her mouth as a toddler. She had a black and white kitten, round and bright as her, which she had also named Peety. It was her constant companion. Gazing up at me, Peety holding Peety next to her face, their eyes became four bright and boundless shafts of innocence examining my soul. There is nothing I could deny her.

When I would assent to her request she would disconnect her gaze, smile a half smile, turn on her heel and seek my equally sympathetic brother to add another favor to a request that I had already granted. "Scotty said he would, but will you...?" If Seth granted more, then she would move on to Mom or Dad. Sometimes I don't think she remembered what she wanted at the start. It was her way of surveying the family to affirm that she maintained her place of special grace and confirm that she had our trust. Which she always had—unfailingly.

Our home was not constant bliss. Far from it. We were bruised by conflict, falsehoods, and distress like every family. Yet, except for one crisis, there had been little lasting trauma in those years.

The crisis had occurred a few years ago with Mom's brother-in-law, Ben. Ben had done the worst thing I had ever heard of, and it is one of those nightmares that revisit a child and infect our perceptions of the world.

What I knew of Mom's sister, Anne, and brother-in-law Ben, I gained in snippets of adult conversation. We had never visited them, but they had been to our house a few times. They lived downstate near Gaylord, and Ben did road work for the county. The burden for their family would have been incredible, living in a mobile home parked in jack pine scrub crammed with four children. Their daughter, my cousin Barbara, would have been about my age. She had severe birth defects, was bedridden, and never left the home. My aunt and uncle had to do everything for her.

My cousins were quiet kids in ill-fitting Goodwill clothes who seemed enthralled with everything in our house and around our property. But their family always had to make the ninety-minute trip home before dark, so they could relieve the elderly neighbor who watched Barbara.

I recall the whispered conversations. The kids dare not interrupt the adults while they talked; Anne sniffling and wiping her nose, Ben's cap brim shielding his eyes as he stared at the floor, clenching his jaw. "Go out and play, Dad's going to make some hamburgers on the grill." Mom would say hastily. "We'll call you." I know my parents carried an enormous burden for Aunt Anne and Uncle Ben and probably helped out more than they could afford.

Then Ben shot Barbara.

In a moment of drunk and tortured logic he just wanted to save his family. He had gambled that a jury would be merciful. But he was wrong. He was sent to prison for seven years and Aunt Anne moved the family back down to Ypsilanti to live with relatives. Mom tried to reach out, but I never saw them again.

"They had to wipe brains off the wall," I heard my parents hiss when they thought we weren't listening.

All my imaginings were worse than if I had been there to witness it. But we all press these things down, pack them away, and go outside and play.

There's more I could say about my parents. My dad was quiet, caring, drank too much, and would come home from work and fade into a portal that passed through the screen and exited out the wall behind the TV. But Peety and Peety would squeeze beside him, and they would watch together in silent camaraderie. I don't think he liked his work. He did not shun the love of his family, but his work seemed to take its share.

My mom was funny. I think she was a little smarter than Dad and he knew it. I would hear her trying to explain their bills to him or discuss something she heard on the news. He would listen carefully until a smile of understanding creased his cheek: often more a smile of admiration than understanding. For us kids, she tried to level off the rough spots; the let downs that came with our childhood. She could distract us away from our disappointments.

It was not always easy, but my life did not seem tragic. At least not in those days.

3

—·—

NEXT SUMMER

AFTER THAT SUMMER WHEN the fairy escaped the berry can and Dee escaped her private world of darkness, I feared I might not see Duane again. Gone for good.

I returned to school where reality claimed another year and summer friendships vanished like swans in a snowy sky. I was resigned that Duane would become another of the fleeting faces of childhood friendships that recede into the murky mix of summer camps, family reunions, and vacation Bible school. Or those *friends-for-life* we've left in vacant classrooms behind the darkened windows of empty schools.

A school year is a lifetime, but friendships that faded in fall can rekindle in spring with a skip and a grin.

After school was done for summer, I couldn't wait to get back to Paradise. Restless after the hour drive, I tore into Grandma's house, skidded into the kitchen, and was instantly embarrassed—and confused.

"Well, there's Scotty. You made it," Grandma said in her usual unabashed tone. "Are you tongue-tied for once in your life? Say hi to your friends."

To me, her kitchen was as comfortable and ordinary as home, so I was not prepared for surprises. I am certain I looked even more stupid than I felt.

"Hi Scotty." It took a moment for the faces to emerge into familiarity—except for one completely unfamiliar face. I recognized the slightly taller and leaner version of Duane. And Dee smiled, even more dazzling in her yellow polo shirt and white shorts. She was prim, assured, and every bit the confident mother instead of the lost girl of her past. But sitting on her lap, pudgy as an autumn plum, was a chubby-cheeked baby. There was a lick of black hair tied with a green ribbon that hovered like a hummingbird over her round head. Dee bounced the child on her knee, her red polished fingers splayed around the baby's belly like holding a ball. The baby sucked at her lower lip while her wide, dark eyes examined me with suspicion.

Duane flipped his hand up. "Hi, Scott." Then without missing a beat, he pointed and grinned from ear to ear. "I have a sister, Gracie!" Spoken with all the glee I remembered. "Hey little lady, this is Scotty," he said, shaking her hand trying to get her attention. But the baby continued to give me a sober appraisal until she looked at my grandma, tipped her head back to look at her mother, then dismissed me with a sideways grin. She batted her arms in the air, noticed Dee's keys on the table, and I was forgotten.

"C'mon, let's go outside. Your grandma said we could use a boat," Duane said.

"I said that you could *sit* in the boat," Grandma said. "Cabin 4 is going to use that boat at noon, so I don't care if you puddle around for a while. Just have it spic and span and tied up by noon. You know the drill, Scotty."

We were out the door as if the previous ten months had evaporated. Duane hurried ahead toward the dock and had drawn the rowboat beside the dock before I was past the racks of beach gear and boating equipment. I grabbed two life jackets and threw them in the bottom of the boat, glancing back at the house. I somehow believed that Grandma had X-ray vision and could see through walls to anywhere that a couple of kids might be trying to have fun without donning all the safety gear she required as someone who owned a bunch of cabins along the wild shores of Lake Superior.

June was too cold for the beach, but most of the cabins were full and a few tourists were milling around near the water. If the lake was calm, Grandma allowed us to take out a boat to fish or explore near the shore. With a few gruff instructions, she had taught me all the dangers, pitfalls, and surly unpredictability of the big lake.

But the water was unsettled today, so Duane and I remained tethered and content to rock in the waves, secured to the dock. Facing each other on the seats, we caught up on all that happened during our time apart. He told me about his schoolyear back in Wisconsin and living with his grandfather while Dee attended school in Green Bay, and he attended the reservation school in Keshena. It was the usual stuff: new friends, senseless school assignments, and the best tricks played on the worst teachers.

Duane paused, his fingers playing along the gunwale of the boat while he looked across the restive waters. He looked at me then quickly away again. "If I tell you something, do you promise not to tell your grandma or any other kids?"

"Sure," I said. After the pain he had endured with Dee last summer I was leery that something bad was happening again. "Are you sure that you should tell me? Will your mom be okay with it?"

"I don't want her to know that I told you. So do you swear not to tell anyone?"

"Okay. I will not tell anyone. Not even my parents."

He scratched his ear. "I think that my mom is someone really important."

I laughed out loud but stifled it when met by the piercing look from his dark eyes.

"I'm not kidding," he said. "Before we came back up here, we had to go to some kind of ceremony at the community building. It was at night, and they burned sage, sang, and drummed."

"Was it a baptism?" I asked stupidly.

"No. Gracie got baptized at a church." He looked across the water as he continued to speak. "This was a tribal thing. I had to be there. We passed the pipe and everything. Mom was dressed in a white leather dress and her hair was all done up. Even Gracie wore a little white ceremony dress," he said, grinning. "You shoulda seen her. She didn't cry or nothing."

"It must've been cool," was all I could think of saying.

"Sure. I had to wear some old dress that I think was my Pop's—"

"You had to wear a dress?" I said, pushing his shoulder.

"No, dummy. A costume: I wore ceremonial dress of some kind. It was actually pretty cool. It was something important. They spoke Native and we were like the center of the whole thing. My aunt took Gracie to bed, I fell asleep, and the party went on all night."

"Was there food?" I asked the only question that seemed relevant.

"Not until the next morning. They woke me up, starving." His face brightened. "There was fry bread, venison, smoked fish, beaver—but I didn't like it. It was greasy. Did you ever eat snapping turtle? They even had turtle stew."

"No. Grandma said she ate snapping turtle. But to me it sounds gross," I said.

"No. It tastes like beef. I liked it." He paused, as though he'd forgotten what he was talking about.

"You think your mom is some kind of Princess Leia now?" I prompted.

"Ha. No, it's nothing like that." He smiled. "It was weird for me. They named her something in Ojibwe. It was Waa...um...Waabishki Oniijaaniw," he said proudly. "The White Doe. Then they gave her gifts, and they treated her special. After that night they treated all of us special."

"Are you a big shot now?"

"I don't know. I don't know what any of it means. When I asked Dee—Mom—she said that she would explain more when we get settled back here. So, I guess I will find out." He turned to me quickly. "You will *not* tell anyone, will you? Promise?"

"Of course, I promise."

"No. Because she also told me to be careful now and not take off alone without telling her where I was going or who I would be with."

"Around here?" I looked around at the dock and the cabins. "What is there to worry about in Paradise?" I asked. We never had to worry about anything or watch out for anything except the traffic on the highway into town.

But, of course, we had never hosted celebrities.

"I don't know. She just told me to be more careful around strangers." He smiled to himself and shrugged. "She is just trying to be a good mom."

Ten months of school and separation evaporated. But he was a different kid somehow. He always seemed older than his years, but now he was more mature, if that were possible. His smile was just as quick and his hair still stood up like a frazzled porcupine, but there was something about Duane that had changed. Maybe he really was some sort of Potawatomie royalty.

There was so much that I could not have known or understood about Duane, his mother, or the mortal forces they would contend with.

"Excuse me, boys, but I believe that this is our boat." A stocky man looked down at us from the dock. Big as a placard, the front of his tall cap read *don't be a dumb Bass* while the sides pushed out his big ears like frog wings. His smile hitched into his cheek to reveal a crooked row of bad teeth. Beside the man were a set of grumpy, plump twins and a younger girl that danced while she pressed her hands into her groin.

"I gotta pee-e. I gotta pee-e," she said.

"Dammit, I asked you guys if you had to go before we left the cabin," the man said.

I said, "Sorry, but my grandma said you wouldn't need it until—"

"Well, here we are. We're twenty minutes early. Big deal, huh?" the man said.

One of the sullen twins, who seemed to be intently extracting his underwear from his butt crack said, "Hey, I have a question."

Duane turned toward me, his back to the dock. He put a hand to his cheek, speaking out of the corner of his mouth, "Well just pull it outta your ass!"

I snorted and a string of snot flew from my nose. I covered my mouth and wiped my sleeve across my nose.

"Hey, I was wondering," the picker continued, completely unfazed.

"What?" Duane said as he pulled the rope back to the dock. I had to look away, unable to control my snickering.

"Are you a Indian kid?" the twin asked.

Duane held his sly smile. "Sure, I'm like the prince of all Indians and my mom is like queen of all the Indians," he looked back at me and raised his eyebrows, goading my giggles.

"Yeah, right," the other twin chimed in. They stepped aside as Duane grabbed the dock and hoisted himself onto the deck. I followed, still covering my mouth and looking away.

"No, he is," I coughed, then had to cover my mouth again.

"C'mon boys, let's get this stuff in the boat while we wait for your sister to piss." The squat dad was already out of breath.

We ran along the dock toward shore.

"I think they was funnin' us," one of the boys mumbled.

With a skip and a grin, running and laughing: Another summer lay wide open before us.

4

Kwak's Korners

Beyond meeting his new sister and telling me about the ceremony in Wisconsin, Duane had one more surprise. He wanted us to meet a new friend.

"Ooo, is she your new girlfriend?" I teased.

"Just one of many," he said with pride and an elven smile. He shook his head. "No, I met Connie only once. She was at our house when her auntie was talking with my mom. Auntie invited me over. Connie made me laugh, it seemed like she might be fun, so I said *sure*."

I began to answer but Duane interrupted. "Oh, and they said that Mr. Kwak built a cool bridge and some other stuff back in the woods that Connie would show us."

Connie was staying with her aunt and uncle at Kwak's Korners. They had cabins and a bakery tucked in the woods on the side of the highway opposite from the lake. They also leased waterfront north of the old cabins where Dee and Duane stayed. It included a boat launch and a strip of beach.

I got the story about the Kwaks from Grandma: Simon Kwak and his wife Doan had purchased the cabins. One of the cabins near the highway was converted into a bakery. Their name rhymed with *dock,* so they were proud to name the new business Kwak's Dock. Most locals knew how to pronounce their name, but tourists were mispronouncing the name and thought the place was Kwak's Duck. The Kwaks realized the mispronounced name was catchy, and people remembered it, so they gave up correcting everyone, and eventually compromised by changing the name to Kwak's Korners. Tourists could pronounce it any way they wanted. But with wit and a wink to the locals, Doan painted a yellow rubber duck on the big sign by the highway. The new name stuck, and the cabins and bakery were a big hit. Both tourists and locals were lined up before sunrise for cinnamon rolls big as saucers oozing cinnamon and dripping butter frosting.

Though my grandma was an ace in the kitchen, she liked to keep a box of Kwak's rolls and doughnuts for the guests on the weekends. She sent Duane and me on a mission to Kwak's. And this would be Duane's chance to introduce Connie.

It should have all ended there.

Careless in our renewed friendship, Duane and I tore onto the highway with our bikes. A blaring truck horn, the deadly howl of braking tires, and a brilliant flash off Duane's bike mirror left me dazed amid smoke and stench from burnt tires and old brake shoes. It seemed minutes lost in this surreal and sulfurous cloud until Duane walked toward me through the smoke, pushing his bike.

Grandma had warned me a thousand times to be careful on the highway.

When the smoke cleared, the truck was gone. Not a trace. It could have pulled in somewhere, but the highway was open as though nothing happened, not a car in sight in either direction.

We were shaken but brushed it off and in moments we were pulling into Kwak's.

We raced off the highway, past the trim little bakery, into a tunnel of spruce trees. I had not been back here in at least a year, but it looked as though the Kwak's had done a ton of remodeling. They always had a nice place, but now everything looked fresh and charming. Further in even the trees seemed bigger, the forest deeper, dappled with swaying patches of light. Chickadees clucked and chittered.

We emerged near the front of the low motel where a line of six red doors were tagged *One* through *Six*. The tourist's cars in the front looked like the round-fendered cars from a century past. Antique auto shows were common in Paradise during the summer, and fleets of old Model T's or Corvettes would tour through town on their way to Tahquamenon Falls or Whitefish Point.

We sped past the neat motel and entered a shaded, dark circle of cabins set in towering white pines. Like a movie set, the renovations were wonderful. The property was manicured, the trim and door frames of the log cabins were painted in bright colors. The office and attached home had been built of stone and had rounded eaves like a fairy house. Slate pathways wound among flower beds, bird baths, and statues. In a clearing behind the Kwak's home, a fence of carved pickets surrounded lush flower and vegetable gardens. Looking around, Duane and I quietly walked our bikes up to the house.

We expected to find Connie or her aunt and uncle.

"Hey, no kids allowed." We heard a girl's voice coming from a window. I looked at Duane, puzzled.

"That must be Connie." He creased a smile and shook his head. "I told you she was funny."

A girl skipped out the door in shorts and a tank top and slipped into a pair of sandals. Her hair was sharply divided into two black ponytails that arched to her shoulders and bounced as she jumped off the steps.

"That's not Connie," Duane whispered to me, confused.

"Who is that?" I whispered to Duane. "I thought we were here to meet your friend."

"I don't—"

"Who's your friend?" the girl asked Duane.

"Um, you're not Connie," Duane said. "I thought Connie was here."

The girl skipped to Duane and tried to shoulder bump him, though her shoulder came well below his shoulder. "Nope, I'm Aaida. Connie will be along—eventually."

She looked up at me. "I'm eleven. And my name is spelled A-A-I-D-A. Don't forget it. Not A-D-A, not A-I-D-A, it's—"

"I think I got it," I said.

She gave me a withering look and studied my face. I doubted she could be more than seven, but she was not someone I wanted to challenge.

"So, hi A-A-I-D-A, I'm Scott," I said.

She offered only half a smile and nodded confidently as though she had been expecting me to say that. Her gaze seemed to look through me for an awkwardly long time. As though she was not expecting to see me or that she expected something different from me. I couldn't tell.

"Is it okay if we go…" Duane began to say, but Aaida was still looking at me. She held a hand up to pause him.

For a moment I was certain her face changed when she said to me slowly, "You boys were not to be here, now. Not yet."

Duane did not hear and continued to speak. "Connie's aunt told me that Mr. Kwak built a cool place back in the woods and that Connie could take us to see it."

I turned to Duane. "Maybe that's not a good idea," I said.

"We won't go there today," she said. "Another time."

"But she said…" Duane said.

"Things are different around here. I will show you the path so you will know how to get there, then we'll turn back," she said. "You will walk that path another time."

"Okay, let's go," Duane said. "Where is it?"

"Leave the bikes, you won't need them," Aaida said.

We flipped the kickstands and parked. Aaida led us into the gardens through a gate twined with carvings. My parents and my grandma have gardens, but the gardens behind the Kwak home looked like something out of one of my mom's magazines. The vegetables were neatly arranged, vines twining around the stems of flowers. I did not know many of the plants and there were others I would not have believed could grow in the U.P. They looked tropical. There was no breeze, yet chimes swayed, tolling deep, sad melodies. There were statues of life-sized rabbits, tortoises, and foxes. Tucked under branches were fairy houses that twinkled life-like.

Duane and I gaped in wonder.

At the back of the gardens was a larger gate carved of solid wood. A sign hung on the gate that said *Do Not Enter.* Beneath this were lines that I imagined said the same thing in many alphabets and languages.

"The trail runs back there," Aaida said, pointing beyond the gate. "We stop here."

"Maybe there is something fantastic back there no one has ever seen," Duane said.

"How do we know if no one has seen it?" I said dryly. "Who cares?" But my curiosity was aroused, too. I really wanted to see what could be yet more wonderful than what we had already seen.

"So what? Maybe it's just a deer blind or place to be alone. Or maybe it's nothing but a made-up story," Duane said, taunting.

This fascinated her. As if no one challenged her. "It is not a made-up story," she said tersely. A moment earlier she was determined we would go no further. Now she thought for a while, looking at the wooden gate, then back toward the house.

"Okay, smart guy, maybe you should just find out," she said. "But I can't open the gate. You will have to do it if you want to see what's on the other side."

"I don't think this is a good idea," I tried to dissuade them. "It would be trespassing, I think."

It was too late; Duane had put a shoulder to the heavy gate and shoved through. I was left standing alone with Aaida watching me, her chin tilted up as if challenging me to follow Duane.

I only shook my head and followed.

For a brief time, a winding trail led through brush and under spruce beside one of the ordinary gullies cut by tiny seasonal streams which in springtime swelled to torrents of melted snow and ran into the big lake. But familiar Upper Peninsula forest soon transitioned. We paused at the top of a steep ravine that descended toward a stream narrow enough to easily jump across. It became more like rainforest than northern evergreen as the banks were covered in ferns sheltered by massive pine and cypress.

The brook widened and plush moss spread over the sharply skewed banks like a quilt. The trunks of the great pines arched upward away from the water to where their crowns spread in haze. Deep ferns came to our waist, then higher. The stream was clear and placid as a garden pond, with golden and silver fish flitting away from shore. A bullfrog jumped from the other side, making a loud *ploink* that echoed in the stillness.

As we went farther, lacey vines trailed from high above and the sounds of strange birds twittered all around us. The stream widened to a pond where lily pads with great orange and yellow blossoms dotted the surface. Duane paused, raising his brows with wonderment and I returned the look. Even the air seemed warmer and more humid as a thin fog leaked among the great tree trunks.

A gloomy awareness swept over us like an eclipse. Duane and I looked at each other again, but Aaida trailing behind, seemed unfazed. We swayed left and right to look past the trees and through the forest. Though flecks of sun were seen through the canopy, it felt like a cloud bank had moved overhead or a shadow was sweeping through the trees. Duane looked around warily and shook his head nervously before taking the lead again, moving slowly along the trail that followed the water.

The bank sloped all the way to the water, so we had to look down, stay on the path, and avoid slipping in.

Duane stopped again.

"Whoa," he whispered in awe. It had been the first time either of us had spoken.

Arching above our heads and spanning the wide stream was a wooden bridge. Its huge posts and slatted rails were carved with peculiar inscriptions and a host of weird animals and strange people. In all our pretend adventures we would never have imagined anything like it. We stepped back to study the engravings of dragons, winged people, and terrifyingly alive masks that leered from the wood.

"We should not be here. I have allowed you too far in," Aaida said behind us.

It started merely as the hoarse cry of a raven several times, then before we could find the source, it grew to a clamor on the opposite bank.

"We must leave. *Now,*" Aaida shouted.

In moments the sounds swelled to a cackling horror of voices from ape-like whimpering to humanoid gibberish. "Hoo hey. Hoo HEY! Hoo Hoo." Then lips flapping, "Br-rweep! Br-rweep. Hoo Hoo Hoo."

Riveted in place, we were frightened by the ridiculous yet terrifying calls, nothing like we'd ever heard in the forest.

"Run!" Aaida took Duane's hand, pulling him back. Strong for her size, she shoved me back along the path.

We ran away as the hideous cacophony came nearer to the bridge. High in the trees on the other side of the stream we heard a rustle and crash and looked over our shoulders to see things black and furry, reeling through the canopy. Not like bears—like apes.

"Keep going, they will not come over the bridge," Aaida said.

The forest exploded in uproar, the creatures apparently howling fury at being barred from the bridge.

Slashing through the ferns, it took only minutes to dash along the pathway and back to the garden gate.

We staggered through the gate, breathless. Aaida placed her hand on Duane's chest. "Never. You must never come here again or try to find that path. I cannot tell you how much danger there can be. I am sorry. I should have known it was not time to show you the way. Not now. It was a mistake."

Duane was nearly in tears. "What was that? What happened?"

"Leave now. Do you understand?" she said. We did not need to be told. Wide-eyed, our heads nodded like woodpeckers.

"Remember your fear and never return."

"What was that?" I asked. "Was it a bear? A cougar?"

"Oh, much worse," she said. "Much worse."

"Is it wendigo? Pops told me stories. But they were only stories." Duane searched Aaida's face for assurance. "Right?"

"It is not that," she said. She sighed and rubbed her brow. "It is not for you to know. Not now."

"But..." I began to say.

She sighed and scratched her brow. "Mr. Kwak would call it Sup-ui namja: Man of the woods. Saseukwachi."

5

— · —

ASLEEP IN THE BOAT

I LISTENED TO DUANE when he needed to talk. A trait I had learned from Grandma Shirley more than anyone else.

My parents would listen to us when we had something important to say. Even Peety's petitions, convoluted and emphatic as they could be, got attention. But despite Grandma's brash nature, no one listened to us like her. If she sensed something was needling one of us she would find an excuse to have us step away with her.

Though the two were nearly opposites, even Peety got Grandma's special attention. My sister's conversation could range from joyous to frantic in the span of a single sentence. Nodding affirmation while Peety rambled on, Grandma seemed as understanding with Peety as she was with us.

Grandma was independent in all her ways, and there wasn't much that she needed help with. But when she knew we needed to talk, she would find a reason for us to help her, and she would listen.

I recalled one day the previous summer while hunkered down with her pulling weeds by the side of the garage. She opened with her standard line: "Well, how's the world treating you?" She reached behind her ear to turn up Grandpa's hearing aids.

"Why do you wear Grandpa's hearing aids?" I hedged, not eager to dive into conversation. "Why don't you just get your own?"

"Well, these are right here," she said. "And your grandpa sure won't need them."

"Then why don't you wear his glasses, too?" I asked.

"Cripes, you're plenty sassy today. Pretty soon you'll have me wearing his boxers, too."

"Eww," I said.

"Well, you ask a lotta questions for someone who is down at the corners of his mouth," she said.

"You started it." I smiled while yanking at a dandelion until I pulled the leaves off. Normally I would be scolded for not getting the whole root, but she tended to be tolerant when listening.

"I wear the hearing aids because he's not here anymore," she said.

"To remember him? So you can imagine you hear him?" I asked, though I knew she was far too practical, and not quite eccentric enough to believe she could hear him.

She huffed. "No. I remember what he sounds like without the hearing aids."

She slid the weed bucket between us. "I wear them because your grandpa was a man who kept to himself. Not because he did not like people. We all know that after the war, it was just hard for him to sort everything out sometimes. He couldn't listen to too much yakking all at once. It made him tired." She drew her hand across her forehead and continued to weed.

I smiled.

"So now he *has* to listen," she said with a sly smile. "No. That's not right. We were like a team, so I guess I only wear his hearing aids when I know there are things he would have wanted to hear."

I raised my eyebrows.

She shouldered me. "Oh stop. I'm not *that* crazy. Not yet! It makes me listen better, too. It's like me and him are listening together, I suppose." She looked up at me, squinting. "You'd have to have been around someone fifty-four years to understand."

I laughed quietly. That was Grandma's wisdom.

"So, how's the world treating you?" she asked again.

After our adventure at Kwak's, I listened as Duane spoke to me.

Bobbing in our favorite retreat, we had left our shoes on the deck and sat in the tethered rowboat. The bizarre encounter at Kwak's Korners riled us so I could not even remember riding our bikes back to Grandma's and finding our way to our refuge on the water.

"Dang! We forgot the rolls from the bakery," I said. "Now we'll..."

"Connie's aunt never mentioned her," Duane interrupted. He seemed troubled.

"Never mentioned Aaida?" I asked. "I thought they were your friends."

"No. I told you I only met Connie one time and I'd never heard of Aaida." He shielded his eyes from the sun while scanning the clouds. "There aren't many kids in Paradise, so I wanted to see Connie again."

"Do you think we should go back? We'll have to get the rolls if Grandma hasn't already gone there."

"I don't know. It was so strange. Everything."

His mind was drifting, as though he were no longer talking to me. "Many rooms," he whispered.

"What do you mean?" I asked.

"Dee—my mom—talks about there being many rooms in this world and in the next. Didn't it seem like another world back there in the woods? Like some place separate and special?" He said no more. I couldn't always keep up, but I was used to some of Duane's ramblings.

Using the seat cushions to pillow our heads, gradually we slid lower in the boat, absorbing the warmth of the sun, the glisten off the water, and the gentle sway of the waves. But I knew what Duane meant. As though we had stumbled into an imaginary world, the forest behind Kwak's was like no place I had seen before.

And I knew we must return.

I drifted asleep in the boat and dreamt.

I had never seen such sadness, not since Uncle Ben shot my cousin. I did not know the source, yet it made my heart break. My grandma sat in her tattered lawn chair at the end of the dock. Next to her sat Dee with Grandma's arm around her. My mother stood behind Grandma with her hands resting on the old woman's shoulders. I had never seen Grandma Shirley looking so old and frail. At the end of the dock my father looked across the water, searching. Seth sat on the edge of the dock with his arm around Peety and Peety.

All the sky was pink from east to west. Creamy yellow thunderheads, their gilded tops bowed in silence, like hushed gods withholding tears, respectful of grief observed. Seagulls dipped overhead but did not call out. The lake was in repose, with scarcely a ripple to break the surface.

Dee stood and walked past Seth and the Peetys toward the end of the dock, stood briefly next to my father, then turned away from the lake to walk toward shore. I had not seen Aaida walking down the dock. Dee was puzzled and seemed to be the only one to notice the girl. Dee ambled toward Aaida, looking back once at the huddled group. With confidence, the girl faced Dee and spoke something I couldn't hear.

In the dream, Aaida seemed older and taller. She could have been my age.

She led Dee along the path toward the cabins where they sat down on a wooden bench in front of a cabin. They spoke earnestly, Aaida emphatically trying to explain something to Dee. Dee listened intently, shaking her head slowly as if in disbelief, glancing from the family on the dock then back to the girl. I could hear none of it.

I looked at Grandma and my parents, concerned and saddened for their deep grief.

When I looked again to where Dee and Aaida had been talking, Aaida was gone. She had left as quickly as she had arrived. Dee was sitting there looking past the dock, over the water, her finger stroking her chin, repeating something to herself over and over.

6

—·—

ON ROUGH WATERS

"**S**COTTY! SCOTT! WHAT HAPPENED? Where are we?" Duane shouted.

As if my mind were dredged from cold depths of the lake, I awoke, the boat rocking violently. "S-sit down. Duane! For God's sake, you're going to tip us over."

"No. We're drifting. What happened?" He panicked.

The bottom of the boat was sloshing, and my clothes were soaked. I wedged myself up, looking into Duane's wide-eyed terror. I peered over the edge of the boat, my head pivoting in confusion. "What the hell?" I yelled.

Like riding the back of a rolling herd of bison, we were pitching, drifting on waves with no land in sight. Each wave threatening to capsize us.

I grabbed Duane and pushed him onto his seat, thrusting a cushion on his lap. "Don't let go of this."

We were without oars, anchor, or life vests, and the boat was tossing and diving, water gushing over us.

I grabbed the bail can floating at the bottom of the boat. Whisking water over the gunwale I yelled to Duane to get down in the bottom of the boat with me. Though I knew little about navigating this cork on teeming water, lowering our center of gravity seemed like a good idea.

Duane threw himself on me, whimpering, his cold hands clutching at my waist while he trembled. He had a steel veneer hardened by life, and I had never seen him panic like this. I threw down the bail can and hugged him. I didn't know what else to do.

"I'm scared. Where are we? What happened?" he stuttered.

"Maybe the boat was not tied down." I knew it was tied down. Clenching his shoulders, I pushed him away. "We hold on, Duane. Someone will find us. They must. We hold on."

We sat in water that sloshed from one end to the other in the little rowboat. I worked the straps of his seat cushion, so it lay across his chest, and I pushed him against the seat at his back while I slipped the straps of my seat cushion around my shoulders. I was losing the battle bailing the boat, but I had to keep trying. If we capsized I knew the water would be too cold to survive for long. It seemed hopeless. Duane used his stiff hands to bail best as he could.

Navigating a turbulent wasteland, I looked up at tumbling clouds that dipped and churned, mirroring the waves. The noise was raw and thunderous; a relentless wet roar tearing at our ear drums. In a tempo from hell, the noise would scarcely recede, then like a great wind it would grow and grow until it crashed over us so loud we could not hear ourselves scream.

A wave hit across the bow and spun the craft sideways. We tipped far right as the boat slipped into a trough so deep we could not see over it. We could have reached out and touched the steep walls of water on each side. Then we were thrown left as we climbed out of the valley to the crest. Foamy tops crashed all around, jostling, rolling, and quivering in a great wash tub of chaos.

As we tilted into the next valley, Duane tried to kneel to adjust his seat cushion across his chest. We hit the bottom of the trough with force, and it threw him nearly over the side. I grabbed for his foot, but it was too wet and slippery. I screamed, "Duane!" but the noise was beyond hearing. He flailed, trying to hold onto the gunwale. He caught the oar lock for an instant just as we were launched up on the back of the next wave. He pitched back, but was nearly flung across the boat to the other side. I caught his waistband and yanked him in and held him.

I would not allow him to leave my grasp. It felt like hours that we rolled and pitched in cold calamity.

But in time, as if swept by a great hand, the clouds lifted steadily and the chaos of waves became a regular roll, though still fearsomely steep for a rowboat. I helped Duane settle beside me on the middle seat and we took in our world again. There was no land from horizon to horizon.

"You didn't have to grab my jeans. I don't want to drown with my ass hanging out." With a level smile, he shook his head. "*Drowned Indian Kid Found with His Ass Hanging Out.* My junior high in Keshena would love it."

"Sorry. But you'll have to get a new ass anyways," I said.

"What?"

"I saw when I pulled you back in. Your old ass is cracked."

He barely gave me the satisfaction of a chuckle. He rolled his eyes.

"What are you? In second grade? New headline: *Indian Kid Killed by White Kid's Stupid Jokes*."

We laughed. It felt good to laugh.

We discovered that by sliding from side to side on the seat we could slightly control the boat. Minimally. It was mainly luck, but the bow tracked ahead so it would climb the wave, crest, and slide into the next trough. The waves had flattened enough that we were almost able to see over the tops when we were at the bottom, but the crests still seemed frighteningly high when on top. The whitecaps whispered and hissed next to the boat, then sighed as we sunk into the trough.

Occasionally we lost our rhythm and the boat twisted sideways. We both held our breath, leaning away from the wave, hoping to keep the water from breeching the side, but gradually we were lifted again, and the bow swung forward as we topped a wave.

Through wave after wave, we twisted and maneuvered until our thighs and backs were aching. Finally, the tiny rowboat could finesse the waves and steered us along with only a few adjustments.

The sky lifted to an even, bright gray. At the top of a swell, Duane pointed far off the bow where a curtain of hazy sunshine swept across the horizon.

"Islands," he shouted.

We slid back into the valley.

"Are you sure?" I asked. Our vision had fooled us several times as mirages of ships and trees had appeared then sunk with the next wave.

"Yeah, look." He pointed again toward the splash of sunlight. Two black specks lay ahead on the horizon. If wind and waves stayed the course, we would drift near.

Duane seemed cheered by the sight. "Toot, toot. Land ho, matey!" He pulled with his fist.

I was still nervous, but it helped my spirits to see the old Duane for a moment instead of the frightened child.

Finally, the waves smoothed, and we were able to take turns bailing. The bow kept straight with little attention. The specks of land were getting closer. What we thought had been islands proved to be the ends of two points of land jutting from a ribbon of shoreline.

The two slender peninsulas stretched toward us, separating like embracing arms—or great horns of a beast. As we neared land, the water had calmed imperceptibly wave by wave until the lake was virtually still. Yet the small craft continued to skim across the surface of the water as though drawn into the cove between the long, narrow points.

I had been here before. To our right was tiny Naomikong Island where my dad and I had ventured while fishing a season ago. It had seemed haunted. It was not much bigger than a small house but was scattered with tin roofing, rotting lumber and the iron stove parts from an old camp. Piles of stones lay like graves.

I was about to tell Duane when he interrupted. "I know where we are. Last summer, Pops and I took a canoe from the Shallows out to that island. Naomikong. He offered tobacco and we left. It's an ancestor place. He said there is a story that anyone who steps on the island is destined to return—and not in a good way."

"What do you mean?" I did not tell him that Dad and I had explored the island.

"Mom and I were not as traditional as Pops—not then—so I never asked what he meant. I just liked being in the canoe with him. I only watched."

The tiny island drifted behind one of the outstretched points of land.

The points were like devil's horns reeling us into calm water of the small bay.

The clouds had evaporated above us and to the west the setting sun slanted across the water, now smooth as glass. Our boat plodded forward by an unseen force.

Duane leaned over the edge, pointed, and gasped. The sun's rays were at just the right angle to cut a sheet of brilliant light through the water beneath us. Under the bow a golden luster rose through sea-green layers. We did not have an oar or anything in the boat to slow us from gliding too quickly to absorb the remarkable scene forming under water.

We gawked in silence.

We were not yet within the small bay, but only across from the ends of the peninsulas that protruded into the lake. Beneath us a world cast in liquid amber emerged as we sailed above in a gondola.

Large water plants are uncommon in the open waters of Lake Superior or in its cold bays, yet here, reaching toward the surface appeared branching, twining trunks in green and gold. Fronds of fern-like foliage spread below us. More remarkable were valleys and pathways weaving through the forest of seaweed. The wreck of a schooner, almost perfectly preserved, slid beneath as we glided above.

"Look!" Duane pointed down in the water.

Gone as quickly as we'd seen her, a woman in a flowing dress waved to us from the deck of the scuttled schooner.

The trunk of an old oak tree stood upright. Beneath a branch that sprouted like an arm, a man with a sailor cap and wearing a striped Brecon shirt pushed on the swing of the little girl he may have left behind when he sailed, her long white hair and pinafore drifting in a slow arc.

"No. There." He looked at me disbelievingly then back into the water. "Near the cave."

A naked giant with face like a troll scowled as he trudged into the cave's black maw, pulling a scow loaded with caskets wooden and carved. The anchor chain he hefted creased his shoulder as the strain creased his brow.

"And there!"

Duane pointed at another schooner deep under water. It was in better repair than the other. On its deck several sailors hovered, working against the waters in slow, liquid movement, securing lines to broad sails that seemed to flow and waver in the clear depths on tall masts reaching nearly to the surface, gilt and glistening in the slanting sun.

We were moving too quickly to be sure of what we had seen. And in a flash the narrow angle of the sun changed, the vision disappeared, and the bottom of the lake rose nearer as we were drawn deeper into the shallow bay.

I was convinced our brief vision was caused by our fright and exhaustion. It had to be.

Our intrepid rowboat sailed on, drawn on the glassy surface until, white as snow, the broad beach along the shore came into view. The forest rose in tiers above the beach from dark service berry shrubs backed by the bright white trunks of birch, slender and graceful as a maiden's torso, upward to the rows of balsam and black spruce pointed and sharp as fingernails, and rising to the great limbs of spicy white pine.

Everything about the beach seemed welcoming and calm after our horror on the open lake. Like a mother's arms, the narrow peninsulas on our right and left embraced us, enclosing us in the quiet bay.

As though we floated above a desert, the white sand lay in stillness beneath us from the beach and spreading far out under clear water. The dusk was not shifting cool, but held warm and balmy like the rarest of warm evenings along the great lake. Smooth as the waters we were drawn over, not a stone or stick was cast on the sands below us.

With a hiss, the bow cleaved the beach, and we paused in a silence so deep it thrummed.

The day was growing dim as the light faded beyond the trees. We were two boys lost and far from home with little hope of finding our way out or finding shelter before dark. With our shoes left on the dock at Grandma's, our bare toes sunk into the warm sand.

Like an orchestra conductor tapping the podium and raising the baton, the familiar chirp of a spring peeper was first to break the silence, followed by a chorus of frogs. Toads lent harmony punctuated by the cello drone of a northern bullfrog. The deeper forest and marshes came alive with the trill of insects peppered with night birds. Moist night air slithered along the sands laden with mossy odors and pine incense.

Duane helped me pull the rowboat onshore. We stood a long while, not sure what to do.

"It will be dark soon," Duane said. "I don't want to stay here."

"I thought I knew where we were. But this seems so different from where my dad and I went fishing. We pulled into this bay, but it did not seem like this at all. It was kind of rocky and the sand was strewn with driftwood and logs. This is not the same." I looked along the beach and at the towering white pine. "Not the same at all. I'd be afraid to try to find our way out."

"If we go straight south we have to hit the highway in a couple of miles," Duane said. Always astute beyond his years.

"I know, but it will be dark soon. I'm not sure what we should do yet."

"Maybe we could just follow the beach. It must take us back to Paradise eventually." He pointed at the peninsula to the west. "We can just cut through there."

Duane was right. If it got dark, at least we would be on the beach where we should be able to walk through the night if we were not found. It would be scary, especially if a storm came up, but it seemed like our only alternative.

"Should we hide the boat?" Duane asked.

"I don't think it matters." I thought for a moment. "No, we should definitely leave it here in case someone comes looking, they'll know where we landed."

We walked to the peninsula that was narrow enough to easily chuck a stone across. Through a grove of cedar, the beach and water on the other side was clearly visible. Stooping under cedar bows, golden leaf-like needles made a carpet beneath our bare feet until a large, twisted cedar trunk lay in our path. Skirting the boughs, we came further out toward the end of the point where a short sandstone shelf cleft the center of the peninsula.

"I hadn't seen this when Dad and I were here before," I said.

We clambered over the shelf, and in the growing darkness, lost our way for a moment.

"That way," Duane said, pointing toward the setting sun.

We edged through the strip of forest, evading several other fallen trees, a tangle of thimbleberry bushes, and another short rock ledge.

"Wow, that was not as easy as it looked," Duane said, laying a hand on my shoulder. He looked up at me with a thin smile. I think we both feared we were not going to be able to walk far after our impossible day.

We came out on the beach. In the dim light, the white sand of the beach made a clear highway for us to follow along glassy waters.

"Should we rest for a minute? Are you okay?" I said.

He shook his head. I knew he was more scared than he let on and certainly more homesick. "Mom will be scared," he said in a small voice while looking down at the sand.

We walked near the water where sand was firmer. The same orchestra of toads, birds, and insects greeted us on this side of the peninsula. I was wary; first looking up to see the wink of early stars, then looking down, while lost in thought and careful not to say anything that would alarm Duane further. It was getting dark.

"No-o-o!" he suddenly wailed.

7

— . —

ANOTHER BOAT

"WHAT IS IT? WHAT did you see?" I asked.

On the other side of the wooded peninsula, we stood in gray light. He pointed, his brows angled in sad terror. Amid the rising trill of night sounds I saw only another boat pulled onto the beach. What did he see? Was it someone from the boat?

"What is it?" I asked again. "I just see a boat."

"That's our boat," he cried.

"No," I assured him. "Our boat is behind us on the other side of the point." My head twisted around, feeling suddenly disoriented.

Duane said nothing as we neared the white rowboat. Fearing that we were not alone, I looked nervously to the darkening line of brush and cedar that hemmed the looming forest.

"It's our boat," Duane said flatly.

I said nothing. He pointed at *Shirley's Cabins: Paradise, Michigan* painted on the side of the boat, then he pointed to two sets of barefoot tracks that led away from us in the direction of the narrow strip of land and cedar forest just like the one we had left behind us. Impossible. The bail can and the same seat cushions lay where we left them. This was our boat.

With the same thought, we turned and ran back along the beach, toward the narrow finger of land that we had just snaked through. Between trunks of scattered cedars, in near darkness, we made out another beach. We stumbled around the dark trunks and pushed aside prickly boughs. Instead of going around it, this time we clambered onto the fallen trunk in our path. Standing on the huge cedar log, there was a moment we could look ahead to see our rowboat where we had landed and back to the frightening mirror image of our rowboat behind us.

Duane placed his hand on my arm, steadying his balance on the cedar trunk and steadying his nerves. It had to be a trick, a mistake.

We scrambled off the fallen tree and followed the beach back to where we had landed. Approaching our boat, it was as I feared: now two sets of bare feet led in the opposite direction toward the darkening peninsula from where we had approached moments ago. Confusing and frightening like a scary clown mask, I didn't know if I felt like laughing or screaming.

The trill of frogs and insects had grown to a wavering shriek. I half shouted from nerves and noise. "I don't know what this is. But it's getting too dark to go on. I think we should haul the boat up on the beach and call it a night." I tried my best to sound like an adult, though I was sure Duane heard the quiver in my voice. I was near tears.

The cacophony of night sounds abruptly stopped. Our ears rang in the sudden silence. It was a clotted calm where not even the water dare whisper. We swiveled back and forth to see what may have silenced the orchestra.

Duane sighed and nervously scratched his head. We waited.

High and thin it began, like a faltering flute, then growing broad and confident, we heard the voice of a girl singing. We spun toward the dark forest where the voice trailed. We could not fathom the words, but the melody swelled sad and longing until we felt hidden sorrows wrenched from our souls, a long journey of triumph overcame our sadness until finally our hearts lilted with the joy of victory.

Beyond the cedars, deeper in where taller spruce and balsam stood, a tiny yellow flame was lit, wavering at first, then growing tall and steady sheltered within a lantern. Several yards farther another lamp was lit, then another, until there flickered a row of lamps at least the length of two box cars. As each flame was lit, a smooth arm, a remnant of gown, or a brief glimpse of the side of a face was traced with gentle light. The voice of the singer followed the lighting of the lamps and when the lighting was complete, the voice sang on.

Stepping through berry bushes the singer emerged into dusky light. Looking across the bay, she continued to sing, disregarding us. Girl or woman was hard to say. Beautiful. Her face toward the sky, she stopped singing, brought her hands in front of her, swept them in a broad arc, hands above her head palms inward like a prayer, then down together in front of her.

She was like the statue of an angel in an old garden. Like a held breath, there was silence all along the beach and through the forest.

Duane looked at me wide-eyed then back at the woman. After half a minute, her eyes turned to the side, a sly smile creased her cheek, and she winked as if it were all a prank.

"You look frightened, boys," she said, sweeping her hands to her sides. Her gown was gray like seamless clouds, and like the clouds, trimmed in silver.

"We-we're lost," Duane whispered.

"No. Not lost. I know exactly where you are," she said. "Follow me. I can help."

"Do you have a phone?" I asked. "We'd better call my grandma, and his mom will be worried. We were on the lake and nearly drowned, and—"

"Nearly drowned," she said. "I suppose others have come here drowned or nearly drowned. All have needed rescue." Though quite young, her smile had the embrace of a mother.

We followed her into the low bushes, through spruce and balsam toward the twinkling lamp light.

As we came near the lights, Duane touched my arm to pause. Each flame was within an amber lamp, the glass wavering like liquid. Intricate bronze brackets, polished and shimmering, secured the lamps to enormous logs that were laid one on the other and running the length of the long porch. Each end of the porch receded into forest and was hidden in pine boughs. Windows with panes of red, yellow, blue, and green were set deep in the logs and shone with a dim luster, inviting us toward mystery.

8

The Lodge

THE LAMP LIGHT CREATED wavering puddles of light and shadow along the broad porch. Deck posts of barrel-sized tree trunks reached up into darkness where countless stained-glass windows, floor upon floor, flickered like fireflies.

Like water rushing back from a parted sea, the night sounds of peepers, insects, and birds flooded back through the forest.

"Come in. We take care of you here," she said.

"We really need to call my grandma," I said. "Where is your phone?"

"There are no telephones here, no television or radio. Nothing will reach us here. We are far from it," she said.

She spoke of phones like she did not know what they actually were, or simply did not care.

Duane was wide-eyed as he blurted, "We saw some people under the water. They were all golden. There was even a giant without any clothes on." I rolled my eyes, no longer believing that we could have seen what we thought we'd seen.

"It is said, 'In my house are many rooms.' You saw one of the rooms, another room awaits within. There are many rooms, and rooms within rooms," she said.

Nonsense. I thought she might not be...stable and I was concerned that Duane would panic—or I would. My mom used to complain that one of my *hippie teachers were fillin' your head with nonsense.* Though I never felt that way about any of my teachers, maybe I understood what she meant.

But Duane piped up. "That's what my mom said." He looked at me smugly, like he already belonged here. "My mom told me about how *there are many rooms.*"

The planks on the porch were wide, smooth, and sounded hollow as we thumped up to the doors in bare feet. She glided gently, her delicate footsteps soundless.

The double doors were twice as high as she, set with windows and inlaid with carvings of harvest: wheat and corn shocks, farmers with wooden pitchforks, women gathering with baskets and old barns with thatched roofs. The scenes were graceful and inviting, and the longer we looked, more detail became apparent. There were mountains, valleys with sheep and cattle. The weave of the baskets, the woodgrain, sweat on the farmer's brow...Duane jumped as, smiling, she touched his shoulder. "We call these carvings *Harvesters Afield.* It is an ancient carving. From fields and forests the harvest is brought to the threshing floors or run through hoppers and past the sorters. So much work to be done. Isn't it all so beautiful? But worry not, we will go inside. We take care of you here."

It was unsettling to be near her. Though her features were not entirely as guileless and pure as her voice, her smile distracted with radiance, and I would have followed it anywhere.

Effortlessly, the girl opened the great doors that glided on silent hinges, then stepped ahead, leading us into a wide lobby cast in soft light. We were embraced by the scent of cedar, old fires, and beeswax. Like a church or funeral parlor, it smelled like a place where people gather but never lived. The décor reminded me of the old log hotels and lodges in state parks we had stayed at. But this room was many times larger than any hotel I could imagine. The furniture was plush: deep leather cushions set in bulky wooden frames. Lamps similar to those on the porch lined the room. From a massive fireplace with a wide hearthstone a fire reflected across the polished cherry floor. The great mantle was held up on each side by identical life-sized ship's figureheads of half-naked women in flimsy wraps. Duane looked away, but I stared too long. They could have been the exact figures of the young woman who accompanied us. And in the light of the lobby, I realized she was indeed a young woman.

I shook my head quickly while scratching my forehead and stepping away, embarrassed. She took no notice. It was not only the figures of the women that had captivated me. There were many other figures carved into the mantle; images of beasts, fairies, and other creatures I could not recognize. Despite my awkwardness, I was drawn to step near again. At the side of the fireplace, a carved figure practically lurched from behind one of the figureheads. The creature was sinister, carved in black wood with simian features more human than ape. I drew nearer, trying to figure out what sort of animal—or monster it was. I noticed the remarkable detail of shaggy fur and impossibly long fingers. The face was...

A glistening eye moved from Duane to me. I jumped back with a yell.

I pointed at the mantle. "What is that? What is all this?" I demanded. But she remained unruffled and unconcerned.

"Sometimes the carvings are so real," she said flatly. "You will wait here until we have a place for you." She motioned toward the chairs and couches. Duane clutched my elbow and I was relieved to be led away from the fireplace.

The lobby seemed to go on forever; endless deep furniture and fireplaces as though a great mirror reflected into an opposing mirror. Away from the fireplace, the room felt uncomfortably cold, but I did not want to be any nearer to the hearth or the mantle carvings.

She touched my shoulder. Though it was only the tip of her finger, the gesture was commanding and firm. "You may sit wherever you choose. This room is comfortable and safe. But the weight of time is deep in some places. It swirls and eddies throughout the house so that guests have found themselves tarrying for too long in beauty, comfort, and..." She smiled, looked around, and nodded subtly. "...rest."

Duane did not hesitate. There were several rows of the bulky furniture running the length of the room, all facing the windows. He plopped into the second row from the windows. The furniture was deep, and he had to reach up to slap his hands on the arms of the chair. I could see he was exhausted, but he seemed expectant, like he was waiting for a show to start. I was not sure what he was thinking.

"Can I call my mom? Oh, I forgot there are no phones." He shook his head forgetfully. "Can someone take us home? I don't think we should wait here tonight. They will be really worried about us.

Especially when they see the boat is missing."

She interrupted our thoughts. "I do not want you to worry when you are here. Your mother is wise—more than you know—and you can be assured she may already know about much of your journey." I could not tell if her smile was reassuring or worrisome: Like she was just making stuff up.

"Do you mean—" I began.

"I do not want you to worry about anything that I say or try to decipher the meaning of my words when you are here. You only need to wait here and soon the way forward will be shown to you."

Now I knew I did not feel comfortable with this woman. The more she spoke, the more confused I became. Without saying more, she left. I swiveled my head to see where she was going, but she had already vanished. Behind us, a long corridor lined with wooden doors stretched into obscurity until the lines of lit sconces on either side of the hall met in hazy oblivion. There was no sound except our breathing and the crackle of the fire.

"I thought she was nice, but she's kind of weird," Duane said.

"Yeah, for sure," I said. Sweat trickled down the middle of my back.

I first noticed it in the floor. It may have been there before, but now I could feel it through my bare feet: a steady thrumming rhythm, subtle at first, then growing to a droning beat. The deep steady back beat was harmonized by a soft metallic whir that repeated over and over in five or six notes. The soft chairs, the low light, and the rhythmic drone lulled us into hypnotic silence. I no longer looked at Duane or he at me. We stared ahead where lamp light flickered through stained glass.

And waited.

I could feel my body. I mean as a kid, my body was just always there when I needed it. I never cared about it unless I was hurt or sick. Even then, it just took care of itself. It just obeyed. But as I sat there, I savored the feel of my breathing, my heartbeat, the cool on my skin. My body worked with precision. I'd always thought air was just forced inside my chest somehow, but now I felt my ribs expand, pulling air into my lungs like a bellows, then relax, pressing air out of my nose and mouth. In, two, three, four. Out, two, three, four. I felt the blood march through my arms and legs with each heartbeat, surging in steady rhythm. I looked at my hand, clenched and unclenched, and thought of the ligaments anchored to a framework of bone, the muscles contracting in opposition to one another to guide my exact movements. I had always felt I was my body, and my body was me. Now I possessed and inhabited this body, this—machine.

On the back of the chair in the row in front of me, I watched a spider crawl along the wood toward a corner of the frame. I did not like spiders, but this small spider was dainty, and its body shimmered like a round emerald. Its tiny eyes were sapphires, and its legs were like delicate, golden needles. It crawled into a corner of the frame, out of sight for a moment. I twitched when it fell from the corner and swung from an invisible strand, catching itself on a strut at the back of the chair. It climbed the brace to the top of the frame and swung itself this time to the opposite side. Over and over, up and down, and across it laid a sunburst of guywires then scuttled on piano fingers back to the center, where all the strands met.

She quietly sat a long time, regaining her strength.

When she began moving again, she worked in small circles spiraling outward. At each guywire she paused, using her gold needles to knit the strand to the guywire, building her circular web: steps and stitches, steps and stitches until the web covered nearly her entire framework.

I scratched my nose. The light of the room had subtly shifted. Mesmerized by the spider, it might have been hours—or longer. She rested at the center of her web a long time again, then proceeded to disassemble the entire web stich by stich, strand by strand. She skittered back beneath the frame and disappeared.

But soon she stepped out shyly again, paused for an instant, and began the entire process over. How many times did the beautiful spider do this? Five? Ten? A thousand times? I lost track. Did Duane see what was happening?

I must have fallen asleep.

9

— · —

DREAM

I HAVE SOME CRAZY dreams. But this one seemed too real; I was a voyeur watching something I should not.

It was like a movie scene, the camera peering through haze and smoke into a small room where a circle of four men surrounded someone in a chair. At first I had in mind an old western where the Indians were convening a sweat lodge before the big raid. But I didn't even know if these were Native men except for the smoke and a muffled drumbeat and singing from a tape player. The men seemed hesitant or awkward, unsure of what they were doing.

And it soon became obvious this was not a sweat lodge, and these were not plains warriors preparing for battle.

While holding a smoking hank of leaves or grass, a man wearing a ball cap leaned over a sleeping woman. He sang something in a raspy whisper while he hovered near her face. She was dressed in a hoodie and jeans and wore sneakers, her feet crossed on a footstool. I was not certain if she was sleeping or if she was merely silent, concentrating on the ceremony.

The other men mouthed the song, one of them tapping the rhythm on a small drum stretched with skins. The smoke circled, the room grew hot and close, the singing swelled, and the drumming was louder. Thump. Thump. Thump.

What I saw next was inexplicable, not part of any ceremony or ritual.

The third man had a white beard and wore a suit coat. He slipped a hand in his coat and withdrew what I thought was a cigarette. I thought he was going to smoke or offer some tobacco, as Duane had described to me. But like a bee—an evil wasp—he smoothly unsheathed a syringe and plunged it into the woman's arm. Hating needles, I flinched.

She startled awake, her eyes wide, brows knit in confusion and her mouth opening in a silent, slow *m-mwah* until her lips were an *O*, her throat open. She screamed only one word: "Duane!"

"Dee!" I gasped. While still bending over, the man with the ball cap swiveled his face slowly from Dee toward me like an owl. He could not have seen me. This was like a movie or a dream that I was watching, so I could not have been there.

When he did not see me, he turned back toward Dee. Her face had grown flaccid, her eyes half open and her lips were parted. The man with the smudge gave a sinister smile to his partners as though they had accomplished something important but awful.

They had killed her.

10

THE WOODSHOP

I LURCHED AWAKE, GASPING, and twisted toward Duane. I thumped the arm of his chair, thinking he might be slumped over sleeping. I reached over, my eyes adjusting to the dim surroundings.

He was gone. I swiveled my head; the vast room was unchanged. The fire was the same, though I had not been awakened with anyone tending it, the whir and droning in the floor continued with the same hum and empty notes, and the light flickered through the stained-glass windows.

Outside, through the windows I saw—snow? Delicate flakes danced, trembling in the stain glass as they twisted downward. The sight unnerved me near panic. We had been at Grandma's as summer was beginning. We arrived here in a rowboat and...I held up my bare foot.

Had Duane wandered off to find a phone or a bathroom? But he would not have left without awakening me and saying something.

I stood scanning from one end of the infinite lobby to the other and down an endless hallway that led away and had been at our backs while we sat in the chairs. Out of sight and distant along the lobby I thought I heard raucous laughter interspersed with comical gibberish, then more laughter, more gibberish. For a moment I thought maybe Duane had found someone…I froze, recalling the sounds. The vocalizations swelled to the guttural cackling and yelps we had heard in Kwak's forest. "Hoo HEY! Br-rweep! Br-rweep. Hoo Hoo Hoo."

With the trampling of muffled footsteps, I dropped into my seat and peered over the side to see the hunched, ape-like figures far away winding around the furniture, inspecting over and under, throwing cushions, and galloping nearer. The creatures would scuttle on all fours, scanning under furniture. Relentless. Their heads would pop up, swivel side to side, their snaggle-toothed, slack-jawed faces wrinkled and hideous, like the creature on the mantle.

I wanted to scream for Duane, but I feared I would draw their attention.

I slid out of the chair, crawled along the floor on hands and knees, then bolted out of the lobby and down the long hallway, grabbing and rattling each iron door handle. Away from the lobby the air was thick, humid, and smelled like the vaporizer that used to spit and hiss on my dresser when I was sick. All the doors were locked. Hallways intersected, each like the main hallway disappearing into haze. I took the first side hallway on the right.

"Hoo HEY! Br-rweep!" And thudding footsteps entered the main hallway off the lobby. Where I stepped along the side hallway, a door on the left stood open a crack, allowing a shaft of bright light to pour onto the ratty carpet. Without a thought, I dove through the door and slammed it shut behind me. I braced against the door, my ear to the wood, the galloping stride and terrible gibberish of the creatures fading.

After waiting several beats, a soft voice behind me said, "Well, hell-o there."

Spinning, I cried out in fear, my back braced against the door.

"Jeepers, didn't mean to scare you, young fella," I heard as I was becoming aware of my surroundings. The room was circled by bright wall sconces and several lamps hanging from the ceiling. A man stood behind a long workbench stacked with wooden boxes, furniture, metal contraptions, and other creations spread across its broad surface. There were benches and tables loaded with tools and a host of mechanical tools connected by belts to a drive shaft along the ceiling. The walls were hung with every sort of rasp, saw, wrench, and hammer ever imagined, not to mention shelves to the ceiling laden with cans of paint and solvent. Rows of jars suspended with lids nailed to the underside of a shelf carried nuts, bolts, nails, and fasteners. The sweet scent of sawdust, glue, and new pine lumber filled the shop. For a moment, I imagined that this was where the thrumming sounds were coming from, but the machines were turned off, and the room was quiet.

The man stepped from behind his creations on the bench and met me with a warm smile. He ran a hand through gray disheveled hair and swept a narrow mustache. He did not seem at all surprised by my intrusion and his attention was more distracted by something he was holding. He continued to thoughtfully stroke his mustache and his eyes averted from me and down at a wooden cup in his hand.

"I think I have it. I think I finally have just the thing." He looked back to me, his lower lip protruding confidently. He shook his head.

"Oh, I'm sorry. I do not get much company here. A new guest wanders in occasionally like you, and that nice woman checks in on me to see if I'm done yet." His brows knit and he said as if to himself, "My goodness, I have been tinkering away in here for a long time."

Scratching his scalp once, he looked back at me and blinked. "And what brings you here, son?" He smiled. "Don't worry." He lifted his hand. "You don't have to answer that. None of the guests seems able to answer that for me. We're all a bit bamboozled here."

"I'm looking for my friend, uh...Duane. Have you seen him? He's eight years old but looks and acts a lot older."

"I don't believe I have," he said. Distracted again, he was looking at the cup in his hand.

"Do you think you can help me find him? I know his mom and my grandmother will be worried. Do you have keys to some of these rooms? A phone?" I thought he might be the maintenance man like our custodian at school.

"I don't know if I have been out of my shop in...in...it seems a lifetime. I have been here trying to come up with the perfect gift for my daughter." With a confident head bob, he looked up at me, grinning. "But I think I finally have it."

The room was a jumble of broken toys, furniture painted pink and yellow, fancy doll houses, bedsteads, and dusty unfinished projects of every kind. Shiny little machines he'd cobbled with gears, belts, propellers, and levers were toppled along the floor. And a few inventions were too convoluted to understand.

"Can you help me?" I asked.

I don't think he heard, but continued to talk to himself. "I can leave now. I know I can leave. She won't stop me. I have it."

He rattled the cup and handed it to me. "When you see Jen, my daughter, will you give this to her?"

"How should I know it's her?" I took the cup. A pencil jangled in the cup with a pleasant hollow-wood rattle. Without answering, he lifted a finger as though he had forgotten something. He took the pencil from the cup and leaned near the work bench to blow a circle in the sawdust. His fingers fumbled in his shirt pocket until he grasped a crinkly piece of yellow parchment. He scribbled a note, then folded the paper and slipped it into the wooden cup. With a wink, the pencil dropped in the cup with a happy clink.

"Oh, and this." From his bench he snatched a big pink rubber eraser like we had in kindergarten. It was worn down and had been used a lot. He dusted it off on his shirt and dropped it in the cup alongside the pencil and paper. "There!" His sky-blue eyes locked on mine. "Will you give this to my little Jen when you see her?" He winked. "I would appreciate it."

Before I could answer he sighed, wiped his hands on his shirt, and looked around his shop as though it was the last time. "It took me so long to figure out the right gift. I always thought she needed so much more."

"Can you help me find my—"

Before I could finish, he brushed past me out the door, looking once left, then continued right toward the main hallway. I looked around the shop in exasperation, hoping for any clue that Duane had been there, then I swiveled and followed him out the door. "How do I find your...?"

And the man was gone. I looked back and forth along the side hallway and I stepped quickly toward the main hallway. I looked back toward the lobby, then the other way along infinite length again. I could hear the rhythmic drone and whir again, but nothing else. For an instant, I worried about the jabbering beasts, but I could see the halls were empty. Where could Duane have gone? The number of rooms would have been endless, with countless intersecting halls creating a web spanning floor after floor: the lodge could be infinite.

My dad, my grandma, or no one at school had ever mentioned this place or the strange cult—or whatever it was, that ran it. When our family drove to Paradise, we would have passed barely a mile from here. Dad would have mentioned it on one of our excursions to Grandma Shirley's.

When I came to the main hallway, I went straight ahead to the other side and stayed in the side hallway. A few doors down another door stood slightly ajar. I thought most likely Duane would have continued down the main hallway and not gone down these side hallways, but I could not be certain. And with these creatures roaming the lodge, I could not waste time. I was frightened they may have already found him.

11

A Very Regal Woman

No longer knowing what to expect, I took a breath and sidled up to the open door. The door creaked as I pushed it wider. Like a mouse, I peered into the room. I should have been prepared for anything after all that we had been through, but there sat another great wonder.

A mound of a woman was wedged by old mattresses into a tall chair nearly wide as a sofa. The chair rested on a low platform almost like a small stage. Her eyes were like two buttons puckered into a face tucked between jowls and rolls of flesh framed by short, black, curly hair. She wore a tattered, gray robe, larger than a bedspread, that was hemmed in red sequins with a brown fur collar. On her head was a fur hat, either too small or maybe it was intended to perch on top of her head like a crown. But it looked like a bird's nest. The wide fur cuffs of her gown matched her hat and collar. If it were not for her somewhat regal appearance, she would have reminded me of those old carnival posters of the *Fat Lady*. As she lifted her hand to her mouth the cuffed sleeve slid back, revealing a freckled forearm larger than my leg. She ate from a plate balanced on her great stomach which she used as a table. Not noticing I had entered, she opened her mouth wide, chomped down on a thick sandwich, and chewed with bovine contentment.

She did not seem surprised to notice me, but merely lifted a finger for me to wait while she looked sideways at me, chewing and chewing, then swallowed. She smiled and raised her small brows. "Don't be shy. Come forward. I am glad you're here." She ran her tongue around inside her mouth and swallowed again. "I am sure you have many questions of me." She swept her hand and sandwich across the room. "You brought me a gift? That was wise of you." She wiped her mouth with the back of her hand, sucking her teeth loudly, and brushed crumbs from her belly.

"I, uh—" The pencil rattled nervously in the wooden cup I had forgotten I carried.

"No need to be shy. I like children. They ask me some of the best questions about myself."

I could think of nothing to say. I had no questions—at least none I felt comfortable saying aloud. I'd even forgotten I was looking for Duane.

Her room was far from regal. It smelled musty and sour. It was set around with sconces like the man's shop. But old barn board covered her walls. Simple, rough shelves were stuffed with hundreds of books. Papers and notepads were stacked and laying everywhere amid dirty cups and dishes. Even the simple desk and wide bed on the other side of the room were covered with more books, papers, and garbage. The only open spot was a small circle on the desk where a pen in a stand and fresh pad of paper sat pristine as a deserted island. A wooden chair, square, wide, and heavy stood near the desk.

"That's where I write all my ramblings and such," she said, pointing toward the desk with her stubby finger. "There is much the world is waiting to hear and much I have to tell them about their foibles and mistakes." Though the pad was empty, and no writings lay nearby.

"I'm Scott," I said. Mostly because I did not know what else to say.

"I am called the Djinn, by some," she said, looking away, pursing her lips shyly, and scrunching her nose. "And some used to make fun of me. But no more." She sighed. "And why would they want to do that anyway? Don't they know?" She looked back to me and smiled. "But you can call me Miss Jenny. Children seem to like that the best. What questions have you brought for Miss Jenny, uh...what's your name, again?"

I scratched my head. "Scott. My name is Scott. Oh. I do have an important question."

She seemed to sit taller.

"Have you seen my friend, Duane?" I asked, then a torrent. "I don't know where he went. We fell asleep in the lobby and when I woke up, he was gone. And it was snowing! How can it be snowing in June? What are those creatures that are howling and running around the lodge? Where'd the woman go who met us outside? Why does—"

"Whoa." She held up her big paw. "Too many questions. I thought you would want to ask about me. Others have just asked boring questions about the lodge, or the planes of time, the rooms above, the world below or the music of the universe. All boring stuff."

I recalled The Church of the Hand of God that was out at the old Air Force base. My mom was astonished when she learned their services consisted of rolling around laughing on the floor in their white shirts and long denim skirts. And my dad told us about a weird cult that lived downstate in the woods north of Ann Arbor who thought the towers of the Mackinac Bridge sent radio signals and that space aliens were going to lift the entire bridge out of the straits and the cult would sail away on the Big Mac bridge to a nearby star. They never missed the Labor Day bridge walk.

I figured that Miss Jenny, along with that entire lodge, was a kook resort. She was not helping my confusion—or fear, but I decided to play along. It may be my only chance of finding Duane.

"What are the planes of time? Why is there—" I blurted.

Her expression flashed dejection because I had not asked about *her*. But she inhaled deeply and dutifully gave an explanation, bored and condescending as one of my teachers reading a social studies textbook ten minutes before Christmas vacation. "You may have found yourself here because you were lost on a pathway that flows through your layer of time. Or maybe you always belonged here. Who knows? Each person exists within a plane, and layer upon layer, the planes of time seem to swirl and mix in this excellent lodge." Pointing down, she said, "On this very spot on the planet, as we speak, there is a Native boarding school run by a Church. Below that, on another plane, Ojibwe are off-loading their Iroquois captives, dragging the women, children and a few surviving men into their village. Above us," Her sleeve fell back as she pointed, "beside a silent beach, the land has reverted to a forest again. We lie *in between* for now and—no one knows what or why." She tilted her head once, shook the care off her shoulder, and eyed her sandwich. "I don't know why. I don't care. And in this room, that's all that matters. Right? Different people from different planes swirl through here sometimes. There are many rooms in this endless mansion."

"How do I find—?"

She took another bite and chewed thoughtfully a moment. But she had been pleased, after all, hearing herself speak. She picked something off her food and flicked it. "Do you think city folks want to slip into a pastoral world of wheat harvest and cow manure? And no matter how beautiful a city may be, would someone who spent their life working on farms and fields, or alone in the forest, want to be tossed into an eternity of shoulder-to-shoulder bustle?" She sighed. "How many times do I have to tell people. Did you think we'd end up at the same station?"

"What the...What are the beasts that roam the halls? They're scary." I said, interrupting loudly. I could not pay attention to her rambling, and I was desperate to find Duane, figure our way out of here, and go home.

She swallowed carefully. She drew the corner of her mouth into her round cheek and looked down at me, tiny eyes narrowed, disappointed that I had interrupted. "The creatures are not from here." She scowled and shook her finger. "And you were not listening to what I was teaching you. The planes swirl and blend. Those things probably spilled over from another plane, another time. Wendigo, men of the forest, call them what you will. They may be from the distant past—or the distant future. Or from somewhere we cannot know. Who knows? Who cares? They are of no concern to me. They are probably seeking new arrivals." She grinned to herself.

"They are—"

"I am sure there is much more you want me to tell you about me and this place. If you will be quiet for a moment, I can probably tell you anything you need to know." Sleeves swishing, she crossed her wrists over her bulk. "The lovely woman and I have had lengthy discussions and she has told me what she knows of the lodge. I had already figured out most of it." She jutted her pudgy chin confidently. "We have hashed over many of the world's puzzles. I am sure she visits me to listen to all I have to say." She paused, thinking. "But the woman is always busy. Like everyone, she listens for a short time and leaves. Yet I have so much to tell everyone."

She knit her brows when she saw the cup in my hand. Then her doughy features brightened. "Is that hot cocoa you have for me?"

I held up the wooden cup that contained the pencil, note, and eraser. "A man in a shop, with lots of inventions and stuff said that if I find her, I should give this to his daughter. But I don't know anyone here and I am afraid I shall never find her."

I had been distracted by her long rant. "Wait!" I said. "*Miss Jenny*—Jen. I remember, now." I rattled the pencil in the cup. "He said it was for his daughter, Jen." Confused, I looked at the cup, then at her. "That can't be you?" I had thought he intended a little girl.

"Let me see," she said cautiously. "What's in it?"

I handed her the cup and her big finger stirred quickly inside the cup like a hen scratching for grubs until she scooped out the parchment note. Unfolding it, her forehead wrinkled in confusion as her lips moved, reading to herself.

She was silent for the first time.

Tilting the cup to see the pencil and eraser, she carefully set it on the arm of the chair. She sniffled, rubbed her nose with the heel of her hand, and read the note again, mouthing the words to herself, then aloud as if telling herself something she needed to hear.

"Written words may abound
Hone and craft, erasing much.
Your every word is not profound
Speak less; listen, touch."

The hand she raised to cover her mouth slid over her eyes as she bowed her head. Her great shoulders trembled, quietly weeping. I said nothing. With a big hand she wiped each eye.

After a long silence she spoke. "My father..." Her voice hitched. She paused again.

"I have been here so long. Sitting here surrounded by my endless life of empty things. I know everything. I lose all control. I have a feeling I've lost control of my life. I am out of control."

I was quiet as I watched her face change like a breaking dam, a tide rushing from shore, or clouds parting after a storm to bathe the earth in sunshine.

She scanned the room. "I know this. I will be ready to leave soon. Not yet. Soon," she said.

She looked at me and leaned forward. Her fingers squeezed the arms of the chair and with enormous effort, she pushed herself up. She teetered for a moment, and I stepped back fearing I was about to be crushed like a bug.

She approached me with shuffling steps.

She pointed back toward the main hallway. "I saw your young

friend. Of course, I was too selfish to listen to him. He was a wise child, so he dashed away immediately when I did not let him speak. Left the door open. He was going to find his mother. I am certain I heard his footsteps down the main hallway, heading away from the lobby."

"Thank you," I whispered.

I was about to turn but saw her sad face. "Will you be okay?" I asked.

"I will be fine now," she said, looking around her sad room. "I will prepare to leave. I must move on. Not quite yet. Soon. Not until the woman returns and shows me what to do. I should have listened to her." She lifted the note and read it again, shaking her head. "I should have known. I should have understood just how simple it is. I of all people should have known."

With slow, waddling steps, she came near and laid her heavy hands on my shoulders, kneading, letting her hands slide to my hands. "You will find your friend. That is how it is. You will find him if you search." She smiled to herself, gripping my hands firmly. "So many nice people have come and gone, yet I have never touched anyone."

She looked at our hands. "I have built upon myself layer upon layer to keep people away. This will change."

12

Where Leads the Lodge

I WAITED AT THE intersection of the hallways amid the melodic drone and damp odor. The hallways were covered in tired carpet that ran forever: a coarse mat patterned of tiny, faded flowers. The walls were hung in wallpaper a gray shade of yellow with thin blue and green vertical stripes disrupted only by mold, water stains, or a peeling edge.

I turned down the main hallway and sprinted back toward the lobby. Though Miss Jenny said she had heard Duane run the opposite way down the main hallway, I checked to be sure Duane had not returned to the big chairs.

But the lobby was empty, the fire still crackled in the hearth, and snowflakes fluttered beyond stained glass.

With a sigh, I left the lobby again and walked the endless hallway that receded into haze.

I tried many doors. All were locked. Each wooden door along the hallways was carved with a different scene: a lovely forest, a countryside, hectic markets, streetscapes, oceans, islands, and more. Hearing a rare, muffled voice or movement behind several doors, I listened, tried the handle, and gently knocked. No one answered. I had to look away from several carvings that were too real, depicting hideously violent battles or that were too confusing and sexual for my young sensibilities.

I wanted to find Duane and leave.

Far ahead, nearly obscured in the haze, I saw someone leave a room, close the door, and walk away. I ran, shouting to them, hoping it was Duane or at least someone who could help. As I drew near, I slowed. This was not Duane.

It was a small man who looked as though he were dressed for a costume party or play. He wore one of those old flat caps, suspenders and a blousy shirt rolled at the sleeves.

"Excuse me," I said. "Can you help me? Excuse me."

He turned at the last second, smiling but confused. "It was always so simple, wasn't it?" he said, tipping his cap. He spoke with an accent. "We could have left at any time if we had only known." His brows knit. "It was always so simple."

I was not sure he knew I was there, but I asked, "Did you see a boy. Maybe this tall, eight years old but he acts older?"

He smiled and shook his head. "It was always so simple, wasn't it?" He repeated to himself.

I slowed, but he kept up his steady pace, and was soon far ahead. Was everyone a nut job, I wondered? Maybe this was not a cult, but an asylum?

It happened several times. I would see someone walking away from me in the distance. When I reached them, they would sometimes regard me politely, smile and nod, but often they did not understand me. If they could speak English, they would always say some nonsense like *Well, it's home now. Pleasant day. Onward and upward. Hoping for journey mercies.* Then they would look away from me as if I were an illusion and traipse forward. Most looked like everyday people, but there was every sort: young and old, many dressed from other times and places, costumes from a school play.

It was like talking to sleepwalkers or to someone drunk. I gave up. Some entered the main hallway from the side hallways, but all were headed the same way down the main hallway, away from the lobby. I followed, hoping I was headed in the right direction and that it was the way Duane had gone.

After hours—or was it days? —I gave up trying the doors, knowing that I just needed to find Duane and leave the lodge. Endless hallways continued to branch off the main hallway and I walked past several broad wooden stairways that curved upward, shadowed in ominous dark. My hopes of finding him were fading.

Everything looked the same and the drone and whir never grew further or nearer. The hallway ahead and behind receded into infinity. I could no longer be sure if I were going away from the lobby or toward it again. Returning to the lobby was hopeless and waiting there until the woman showed up frightened me. I did not want to risk falling asleep again and I certainly did not want to see those creatures.

I was close to tears. I cried a little, feeling lost and hopeless. I was ready to collapse, give up, and sit on the floor watching the sleepwalkers shuffle past. Door after door, hallways branching off hallways and stairs twisting away into nothingness. I was lost and helpless.

Passing another of the intersecting hallways, I looked each way, but I knew it was futile. Still, it was not possible that the lodge was infinite, and I would not allow myself to admit that I may not find Duane.

I decided I would take the next stairway, despite how frightening it may be to venture into darkness with the ape-creatures running about. If I went up the steps to find the top floor maybe there would be a balcony or an outlook. The upper stories may not be the same as the main floor. I brushed aside the thought that the stairs may go up forever like the hallways. That was impossible. No place could be infinite. *Yes. I just got lost and turned around. I must have just—*

"Scott!" I ignored it at first. I was sick of apparitions and nonsense.

"Scott. Why won't you stop!" Duane sobbed.

I turned to find Duane, near collapse plodding behind me, his face washed with tears. He stopped and rubbed his eyes with a fist.

"You wouldn't stop," he cried.

"I...I didn't see you. Where were you?" I asked.

"I was right above you." He pointed up. "I was on the ice, and I could see you walking down the hallway beneath me. I was on my knees pounding on the ice until it cracked, but you didn't look up." He wiped his nose and continued. "Then you were walking on the ice above me. I shouted but you never stopped. I saw cracks in the ice, and I thought you would slip, or the ice would break, and you would fall through. Then I was above you again. I don't know how I got there, but as soon as I saw you I followed above you. I came to a place that was all cracked and jagged and I fell through with a crash. You must have heard *that?*"

I shook my head, confused and not sure I believed him. He may have been sleeping and dreaming somewhere. "I've been walking down this hallway forever. I never saw you. There was no ice, only endless hallways. Where were you?"

"I just told you," he whined. "I just said—" He stopped speaking. Confused, he pointed down the hall.

I turned to see to see a small person far down the hallway. Not shambling away, but leaning against the wall, arms folded, looking at us intently.

"C'mon," Duane cried. He grabbed my wrist and pulled me toward the figure.

"Wait, Duane. They don't know anything. They can't help," I said.

He looked at me like I was being ridiculous.

"It's her!" he said.

And it was.

Aaida unfolded her arms and put hands on hips, her lips pressed tight as she waited for us

"Where do you think you're going?" she said as we approached.

"Are you lost, too?" Duane asked.

"How did you get here?" I said. "We have been here...forever, I think."

She looked older again. Possibly even older than when I had seen her with Dee in my dream. She was tall as Duane, though he did not seem to notice the difference.

"This way," she said with a tilt of her head.

We walked to where the next hallway intersected. She tilted her head and led us down the side hallway.

"Shouldn't we stay in the main hallway? That's where everyone else was headed. Maybe that's the way out of here."

"You do not want to go that way," she said without turning around. "Not now, not *together* anyway."

There was no more conversation, no explanations, waving off our slew of questions without a word until she paused at a darkened stairway. Instead of curving away upward into gloom, this one wound only downward into darkness. I had never thought of walking farther down the side hallways, and I did not want to go *down* into the darkness.

She stood with her open hand, offering the way downward while the other hand scratched her forehead impatiently.

Duane looked from her to me shaking his head, lips drawn, and forehead wrinkled in worry. "I don't think I want to do that." He folded his arms.

"You will find that it is the only way for you," Aaida said.

I stepped onto the first polished oak step and grasped the smooth, sculpted railing. A smell like wet rags wafted up from the darkness and it seemed the melodic whir and drone were louder below in the darkness.

"Turn right when you reach the bottom. The very bottom. A dark creek will take you—"

"Home?" Duane said faintly.

"The dark creek will take you to a wilderness of delirium—eventually," she said.

Duane rolled his eyes and breathed through his nose in resignation. "Oh sh..."

"Wait," I said. "You're not coming with us into this...this wilderness?"

"I can't. Not here, not now." She sighed. "I may see you again, but that is not up to me."

I started down the steps. Hand shaking, Duane gripped my arm.

"I don't want to do this," he whispered.

I laid a hand on his. "We're out of options. Aaida seems to know more than we do."

She seemed impatient. "Don't get lost again," she said. "Go down as far as you can, or you will be lost again, wandering forever."

"Where does this—" I turned to ask.

"Turn right at the bottom, and don't stop until you find the creek through the cave of the final song. There may be others there," she said.

"Others? What do you mean? Other *what?* Like those things up there?" I turned to ask.

She was gone.

"Aaida!" I called. I went back to the top of the steps, looking each way down the hallway, but she was nowhere in sight. I returned to Duane, shaking my head silently. We had nowhere left to go.

13

THE UNDERWORLD

WE HESITATED, LOOKING DOWN into darkness. Who was she? Why was she here, and why had she left without another word?

"She was talking to your mom, to Dee," I told Duane. "I had a dream—at least I think it was a dream."

"Aaida was talking to my mom?" he said.

"Yeah, I couldn't hear what they were saying, but she seemed to know something, and your mom listened carefully to all she said."

"Why is she older, now?" he asked.

"You mean Aaida?" I said. He had noticed, too.

He nodded, looking into the depths.

"I don't know," I said. "Maybe we didn't really notice her at Kwak's place, or we forgot what she looked like after everything else we saw there." It was a lame answer, but I did not want to frighten him further. He was already confused and scared.

There was no reason to go back up the stairs. We had been in the lodge for hours—or days, or weeks it seemed. Maybe this was the only way out of here. Aaida seemed to know what she was doing and had led us straight to these stairs.

But now she was gone.

We stepped slowly, step by step, Duane clutching my arm. Though I felt like I wanted to clutch *his* arm. He had always been the adventurous one, calling the shots, and deciding what we would do. The drone and whir grew louder for a while, as though it lay beneath the floors of the lodge. Then it receded to silence the further down we ventured. We arrived at the bottom of the first flight, but the stairs turned and went further down. We paused on this floor.

"She said to go all the way to the bottom," Duane said, letting go of my arm. He had recovered a shred of his usual confidence, but we were both nervous as we looked around.

We had come to a floor much like the one we had left above, except it could have been vacant for decades or more. In damp air, the striped wallpaper drooped from the walls like fronds. Peering around, the rotting carpet squished as we stepped into the hallway. There were scattered sconces, a few broken but lit, lending an eerie twilight to the hallways. Several of the doors stood ajar or off their hinges. Most of the carved scenes were moldy or worm-eaten beyond recognition. The darkness behind the doors was blank and restless.

I stepped into the main hallway and each way I looked soon faded to black. Without the mechanical thrumming, it was utterly silent for a moment.

"Let's go," Duane said in a small voice. "She said we should…What was that?"

Far down the hall we heard a sound at first not more than the whining of a mosquito or the thin mew of a kitten. Then behind us and all along the hall the sound was mirrored. Thin, hopeless weeping; more voices joining the soft chorus of agony.

I edged down the hallway to a room nearby where one of the voices trailed.

"No!" Duane said. "Don't. We can't stop now."

The door hung by a single hinge, the darkness within the room impenetrable and the thin whimpering came from deep within.

"Hell-o," I said. My voice hoarse and strangled.

Far in the room I could make out what I thought was someone slowly rising. In the gloom, I thought they held a gray cloth or towel in front of their face. I edged backward as I heard shuffling, but I could still see only the narrow gray wavering toward the doorway until it emerged into the murky light.

At the edge of the darkness appeared an impossibly long, gray face, all the features melting in sadness; the eyes long, empty slits and the mouth down-turned big as a horseshoe. The face slowly turned left and right as it floated near, as if struggling to release itself from the darkness of the room. Though gray, wrinkled lips did not move, mewling sobs slowly grew to a slithering wail.

I bolted, grabbing Duane's wrist, ran back to the stairs, and plunged down the steps. The next floor was more decayed than the one above. We did not slow but turned the corner and scrambled down the next flight. We were halfway down, nearly breathless before we stopped.

"What did you see?" Duane asked.

"Uh...well... it was...I will tell you later. I have to think," I said between breaths.

"It was just sad." I finally said mainly to myself, unable to shake the haunting. "Just sadness."

Duane looked at me and blinked, not wanting to know more.

Further below, the *plink, plink* of dripping water echoed as if in a cavern. As we continued downward, a dull, greenish light emanated upward. Our eyes had phased into adjustment, but we could not discern the source of the lifeless glow. Our feet grated as the wooden stairs had transitioned to stone steps. We stopped to listen several times but heard none of the terrible weeping, only the steady drip of water.

The flight of stairs was longer than the ones above and began to turn back on itself in tighter curves until it was no more than a cramped spiral stairway.

We edged down, our hands bracing the cool, damp stone.

At the bottom we came to a landing barely larger than a closet. The staircase did not turn and go down further. A low, narrow cavern led away in both directions. Greenish phosphorescence marbled the walls and reflected a wet path. The scent was no longer the moldy rot from the floors above, but earthy, like moss and pond water.

Set in the same pattern as the hallways above, arched doorways yawned dark and lined each side of the cavern.

"I don't want to. I don't want to do this," Duane whimpered.

From somewhere, I found resolve for him. "We have to, Duane. We turn right until we come to a creek. That's what Aaida said. It's our only hope. We can't stay above with those weirdos and those creatures, and we must find..." I did not want to say anything or even think about a wilderness of delirium.

I turned to look back up the steps, but it was completely dark. Not only dark, but it was as if there were nothing there. With Duane right behind, I circled back up a few steps. The darkness became heavier, almost liquid; impenetrable and oppressive. Like a heavy shroud, I could not reach past it. It loomed, pressing us back down the steps.

"We can't go back," I said firmly. I could not allow Duane to see my fear. I had to be strong. I felt like I was being like my brother, Seth. I no longer felt thirteen years old. "Aaida said to turn right, so that's all we can do. I don't know how she would know, but—"

"I don't like her, and I don't trust her. Why is she here? I was scared at Kwak's Korners and I am scared now. Wherever she is, it's scary. I just want to go home," Duane said. But in a moment, he wiped his nose with the back of his hand. He sighed, blinked, and stuck out his chin. "But I think I am ready to go on if this is the only way out of here."

Duane seemed older, too.

The coolness of the stone felt refreshing after the heavy humidity of the hallways. But we still had bare feet and walking far on moldy stone would be difficult. And if it was truly snowing outside in this crazy world, how would we manage if we ever found our way out of there?

The cavern stretched into darkness, though the glowing walls provided just enough light to walk without tripping. The doors on each side of the cavern were spaced the same as the doors in the hallways above. I touched the moist wall and swiped across the swirling patterns with a finger. The glow came from gleaming slime that I rubbed between my fingers and held up to Duane. He smiled, curious, and dipped his finger to withdraw a shimmering glob. Streaks of red and blue glittered in the ooze, and it had a scent like cedar.

Neither of us wanted to walk past the gaping doorways. The eerie glow spread into several of the rooms casting them in pale light. And seeing what was in these rooms might be even scarier than if they remained dark. We peered cautiously into the first room. It was the same size as the rooms in the hallways above where I met Miss Jenny and her father. Pieces of decaying, ancient furniture were sagging into the floor as if melting. A heavy chair with wooden arms, listing like an old man trying to rise from tar. What may have been an antique couch or a bed with large posts hulked like a rotting carcass. We inched on.

The entire cavern was wet, and the ceiling seeped, but from the next room came the source of the constant dripping. We stepped closer to look in. The room had none of the rotting furniture. Only a long, open sarcophagus, cut of stone, jutted from the far wall. It had filled with water, and from a hole in the ceiling, a steady drip fell into the pool.

Duane drew a startled hiss and squeezed my arm. In the water bobbed a creamy dome the size of a skull, flecked with moss. Expecting a putrid eye to roll toward us any moment, we hurried away.

We listened at each door before peering inside and sneaking past. Most rooms held more rotting furniture or stone platforms. After we passed several of the musty rooms, Duane gathered a bit of courage and walked ahead a few steps. Until he looked into a room and stifled a scream.

I grabbed his shoulder and pulled him back. He mouthed, "Don't. Don't look."

I had to.

In a room as dreary as the others, the furniture was dissolved and sagging. In a corner was a stuffed chair listing to one side. It sprouted mushrooms and flowing white filaments. I gasped when I understood.

A skull perched amid white hair; its bony fingers spread on the arms of the chair, blackened eye sockets staring.

I began to whisper to Duane, "It's just..."

The head moved back and forth, slowly back and forth as if in regret. From between skull teeth in a monotone whisper, "No...No...No..."

"Run," Duane blurted.

Slipping and stumbling we approached a tall, black archway. Two steps led downward, but the glowing slime of the hallway did not follow around the sides of the archway. Like the curtain of darkness on the first flight of stairs it appeared impenetrable. Duane grabbed my arm. "I hear breathing." But I ignored him. I did not want to hear what he said. We jogged past, too frightened to linger. Aaida had said only to go down as far as we can. This was far enough.

It chilled me to ponder whether this cavern and all these rooms had been occupied long ago. It was as if the entire floor had slowly sunk below. How many floors of damp caverns, haunted rooms, and horror stretched into sinister darkness beneath us? I recalled Miss Jenny describing layers upon layers, planes of time stacked one upon the other. But it was hard to imagine that this was what she meant.

My dad told me there had been an old boarding school near Naomikong Bay that was restored to a hunting lodge before it burned down in the early 20th century. But that was like a schoolhouse built of wood. I did not believe there had been anything like this lodge. Never.

"Look," Duane said with the hint of a smile in his voice like I had not heard in ages. He had gone ahead a short distance, and I looked up, hoping we were closer to the end than it seemed. But he was pointing through one of the arched doorways. I could not imagine finding anything here he would be happy about and I was concerned for a moment that poor Duane might be growing delirious.

"Look, Scotty." He pointed with a broad smile.

Gazing into the room, I did not know how to react. Like Duane, I was trusting Aaida less and less, and I could only shake my head in doubt.

"No, wait. Don't go in." I grabbed his shoulder.

"Why not? It can't be any crazier than anything else we've seen here," he said.

That's what I was worried about.

This seemed wrong. He shook off my grasp and stepped into the room.

The room was washed with clear, white light that radiated from the top of a stone pedestal. I thought a lamp burned beneath a metal shade or helmet. But it was not a candle and not a helmet.

On the pedestal, planted as proudly as we had seen a year ago, glowed a white sprout with leaves folded coyly like tiny wings. Above the sprout floated the berry can, a bit rusty and battered the same it had been before Dee restored it.

"No, Duane. It's our imagination. Don't."

"I'm not going to touch it." He sounded incredulous. "It will go away if you try to touch it. It's bad luck."

I clutched his shoulder. "Don't," I whispered.

Duane looked at me his brow knit in disappointment. "You don't have to be afraid, silly head. We will be all right, now. I know it." He continued to stare in wonderment, his face aglow like a child seeing his first Christmas tree.

"Make a wish," he said grinning.

14

LIGHT AT THE END OF THE TUNNEL

WE WERE DISTRACTED BY the rumble of tumbling rocks; a hollow clatter like coconut-sized stones. We rushed from the room. The sound had echoed from where a distant point of gray light fluttered and widened across the ceiling. Though the light was weak as a dim bulb, it reflected off the damp floor and walls to form a shimmering pathway. Was this an escape or another hazard?

To investigate, we would need to creep past countless of these dreary rooms that could hold anything from appalling darkness to the howling man-beasts that roamed the hallways above.

Duane sighed with resignation. He drew upon maturity I had not seen in him just a short time before. I placed my hand on his shoulder as if to ask, *are you sure you want to do this?* He merely shrugged. *What's the choice?*

Fear hurried us until we were running past darkened arches, not looking left or right. Each gloomy room made us more frightened until panic clawed at our heels. The faster we ran, the dim light from the ceiling seemed to stretch farther from our reach.

There is a point where panic squeezes our senses into sheer focus and surges to mindless courage.

That is how we nearly collided with a miserable threat.

Duane grabbed my arm. Not just grabbed my arm, he yanked me backward, our bare feet slip-sliding on the slimy floor.

With his face frozen in fear, he pointed silently a few feet ahead, where lost in the swirl and gleam of murky light, a mass of glowing horror hung like a Chinese lantern left out in the rain. Across its surface, features swam like distorted faces.

"What the...?" I began to say.

More curious than frightened, Duane tiptoed nearer to the hanging mass. I hissed for him to get back, but before I could reach for him, he shouted, "Bees!"

I hated bees. But I was too close and too frightened to run. I froze. The growing rumble meant they were already agitated. And crawling over the surface of the nest were not ordinary bees or wasps. Each was big as my thumb, fat and gray like grubs with short wings that balefully buzzed in the silence of the cavern.

We backed away.

"What do we do?" Duane asked while looking back from where we had come and forward toward the light. More of the thick insects were pouring over the nest.

"Maybe they can't fly. We hadn't seen anything flying around before we saw the nest," I said.

Duane lifted his chin to where several of the fat creatures crawled onto the ceiling, making their way toward us, while others crawled down the wall toward the floor. He squeezed my arm. "I think we should go for it," he said. "We have to reach that light. It may be our only way out."

I wanted time to think about it some more, but I felt Duane would bolt if I hesitated. I was afraid he would run back along the dark cavern toward the room where he'd seen his faerie.

And he bolted— but toward the light.

"Duane, no. Stop!"

The bees had reached the damp floor. He hopped over a few of the creatures and kept going. Several more plopped from the ceiling, and he yelled, smacking them away as they hit his shoulders. "Ugh!"

"Are you stung?" I asked.

"No, they're gross." He was already on the other side of the nest and running. "C'mon," he shouted.

I closed my eyes and took a deep breath. Along the rocky ceiling and damp floor, the bees streamed from the nest.

"Run!" he shouted.

I darted, hopped, and twisted. "Eww, yuck," I said, squishing with bare feet. I waited for the searing pain of a sting, but luckily it never came.

"Keep going," I shouted when I caught up to him. I grabbed his shoulder to keep us from stumbling and we tore ahead.

We ran until we were near the light. I prayed more rocks did not fall and seal us down here with those horrible bees and any other underworld creatures.

We slowed to a trot as we approached and could see where the light was coming from. We clambered over the pile of rocks and into the murky light.

Above us was a ragged opening seamless and gray, no bigger than a barrel. Dim light filtered into the tiny vestibule where we stood on top of the heap.

I groaned. I had hoped we could crawl out and find a way out of here, but the hole in the ceiling was far out of reach.

The cavern we were in continued on past the heap of stones, with more of the black, arched doorways receding out of sight. But the way ahead was absent the swirling phosphorescence that had lined the cavern and the rooms behind us. The ceiling had opened at an intersection and another dark cave branched away to our right and left, darker and craggier than the one we were in.

The rocks had fallen onto a sort of natural bridge that arched slightly higher than the floor of the cave we had been in. But it was still not high enough for us to reach the opening above. Flowing through a conduit under our feet and travelling along the crisscrossing cave was the sound of trickling water echoing through darkness.

"The dark creek," I said. But if it was the creek that Aaida had mentioned, it crossed beneath us and stretched away from the cavern pitch-black in each direction. It would be impossible to navigate darkness next to a slippery creek. She had only said don't stop until you find the creek. "Did she tell us to follow the creek? I can't remember. Or did she somehow know there'd be a hole in the ceiling for us to escape through?" I asked Duane.

Distracted, he didn't seem to care.

The ragged hole above us was too far to reach; at least three times our height.

I was despairing, but Duane stooped and chuckled. Balling something in his hands, he pitched it. Snow smacked my forehead, cold and bracing. I had been too distracted and disheartened to even notice the gauze of snow beneath our bare feet. It must have dropped in from overhead with the stones. Snowflakes continued to sift downward in pirouettes and twirls, the light above showing each flake as it melted on Duane's smiling face.

Above was our hope. If we did not find a way to get there, we may wander in this cavern until we died.

The only thing I could think of was to turn around and peer into a nearby darkened room in hopes of finding any scrap of furniture to pile under the hole in the ceiling. If we could pile more rocks and then stack debris on top maybe we could...

But Duane tugged on the back of my shirt and pointed down the side cave where the creek ran away from each side of the main cavern. There was a shuffle and the rattle of small stones. I put a silent finger to my lips and stood beside Duane, squinting into shadow. Prepared to dash, we listened. The sound stopped. A low burbling whine made the hair on my neck stand up. The sound came again. *Whaa. Whaa.*

"The creatures," I whispered.

But Duane shook his head and held up a hand.

The shuffling steps resumed. Blubbering and other odd noises reverberated in the cave.

"Let's go," I hissed.

But before I could scramble off the pile of rock and snow, Duane grabbed my elbow and pointed into the darkness, shaking his head slowly.

Through the darkness the vague form of a figure in white moved slowly and confidently, picking its way cautiously, not scrambling crazy like the man-beasts. It took a while for the vague form to take shape.

A small woman not taller than Duane stepped out of the darkness and stopped. She looked up at us, watching unconcerned from beside the creek that flowed along the bottom of the intersecting cave. As she turned to look back at where she had been, an infant with red cheeks and a face round as a plum peered wide-eyed at us from a cradle board. The infant took fingers out of her mouth, smiled crookedly, and knit her brows intently while babbling, "Mum, mum, mum." Then she smiled at Duane while babbling and blubbering some more.

The woman could have stepped out of a movie set or the pages of one of my American history books. Over her white dress was draped a heavy white leather robe trimmed in fur. She had leggings up to her knees tied with crisscross leather strips. From her feet to her shoulders her clothing was adorned with intricate bead work, pieces of shell and glittering silver. The infant's hair was tied up in a tiny spray with a silver ring and her cradle board was decorated with beads and carvings. The child was also bound in delicate white leather. For her amusement, ornaments and little dolls and animals made of fur and leather hung from the handle of her cradleboard.

The floor of the cave where the woman stood was well below us. She was not fazed by our presence. She offered a hand and before I could protest, Duane gleefully scampered down to help her up. As she neared, her scent was strong of woodsmoke, sage, and tallow. Her manner conveyed calm assurance; an island of serene hope amid the world of unreality we had experienced. With a placid smile creasing her face, she looked up to me then over to Duane.

"The fairy in the berry can answered my wish!" Duane said like he was ready to hug her.

"I don't know, Duane, this could be…" I still had to be wary. But I didn't know what to say because I did not want to destroy his hope. I understood Duane missed his mother and little sister, but this was not Dee and Gracie. This could be another strange inhabitant of the lodge. I was not trusting anyone or anything in this dreamworld.

After coming out of recovery, Dee possessed that sort of feral beauty that even someone my age could appreciate. This woman was stout, shorter than Dee, but her demeanor was similar: steady and unfazed. And the child was younger than Gracie.

The woman slipped her thumbs under the strap that anchored the cradle board to her forehead. She pushed the strap up and over her head. Duane fearlessly stepped up, and facing the infant, grasped each side of the board. The little girl stared up at him wide-eyed, "Mum, mum, mum."

"She's hungry," Duane said.

He helped the woman remove the board from her back. She turned to take the bundle from Duane and settled it on the stones away from the snow. The child looked disappointed to leave Duane.

A bag was slung on the mother's shoulder. She slipped it off, and after untying two straps, she handed it to Duane. He looked at me and I shrugged. She nodded. He reached inside and removed rolls of soft leather and fur. She nodded again and pointed from the material to each of us. Shaking out the rolls, we found gray leather leggings and rough tunics. Two pairs of moccasins fell from the rolls.

With her lips the woman pointed at the clothing again. Duane and I looked at each other. She pointed again with her chin into the darkness that followed the stream leading in the opposite direction from where she'd come. We had few choices. We could not continue to stand in the snow or walk along damp, moldy caves in T-shirts, jeans, and bare feet.

While we pulled the leather over our clothes, the woman had unlaced the baby from the cradle board and sat on the stones nursing contentedly. My clothing fit well, but Duane's had to be rolled at the cuffs. Grinning, the woman pointed to laces on the moccasins that tightened to fit his feet.

Duane sat down next to her, and the woman glanced at him with a smile. He smiled up at me.

What—or where is next? I wondered to myself.

15

—·—

THE DARK CREEK

T HE INFANT SLEPT THROUGHOUT the bustle of lacing her into skins again. Her head lolled to the side, her tiny mouth open between mounds of round cheeks chubby as a tadpole. With the child secured to the cradle board, Duane helped the mother swing the bundle onto her back and secure the strap over her forehead. The mother smiled her gratitude. We stepped down into the dark cave that led away from where the woman and infant had come. In moments, we were cloaked in darkness and shrouded in silence except for the gentle scuff of her moccasins and the trickle of water beside us.

Around the Great Lakes, scoured and crushed by glaciers, natural caves are uncommon. With my dad we had explored the area around the Fiborn Quarry where, in deep ravines, lay the opening to limestone caves posted with warning signs: off limits to exploration. They are the longest caves in the state, but too torturous and treacherous for anyone but seasoned spelunkers. I hoped we had not found our way into these long and dangerous caves.

We braced a hand against the smooth, cold wall to keep from sliding into the rivulet that ran along the floor of the cave. Though free of obstacles, the path under our feet had been worn slippery smooth. The moccasins gave our feet grip and the leather clothing kept out the cold damp. In darkness, I stretched my hand in front of me to avoid any low-hanging shelf, but the cave was wide open and clear. The steady shuffle of the woman's moccasins lulled us into a rhythm.

Lost in thought, time escaped until we sloshed through another cold creek that fed into the cave from the side and created a larger stream for us to navigate beside in darkness. We walked slower as the small river became more serpentine. Our footsteps and the resonating burble of running water told us the cavern was widening.

Duane had not spoken but followed the woman in contented trust. Given to chattering when he could, he was just as likely to fall into these long, thoughtful silences.

A few steps beyond the convergence of streams I felt a steady draft tease the back of my neck. It was not like a breeze shifting and fading but a steady force that grew until I nearly lost my footing. Ahead, I heard Duane stop for a moment. I was certain he felt it too.

"What is...?" he began.

I steadied myself, bracing my hand on the wall.

Then we both heard a whispered note that carried gentle as a flute. It rose to a melody far behind us coming near, very faint and hard to distinguish from the sound of the draft that pressed steadily at our back. Then a voice drifted past, suspended in air like a presence: the delicate song of the woman in the lodge.

"*We dreamed our dreams and died.*"

I swiveled my head, trying to force my eyes to see in the dark, not certain if I'd heard or if it only played in my mind. I thought she sang another language when she first sang, but now every word imprinted on my brain.

"*From great endeavors and brazen transgression.*"

Then I recalled Aaida's final words—the cave of the final song.

Another line drew near and slipped past.

"*The heart of humanity desperately broken.*"

I felt Duane touch my arm and we stood silently as more song washed over.

"*No image shaped with hands or name spoken with a voice of flesh.*"

Then one line flowed after the next:

"*No heart finds rest.*

All humanity disparages its ancestors.

Until the living overtake the living.

Only the dead prevailing.

The shame of broken love and betrayed embrace.

Like a black earth it covers the moon.

Lies eclipse the truth.

Greed steals the treasure.

As pride steals the soul.

We dreamed our dreams and died."

It was too much to fathom as the song flowed past like a river. But I somehow felt broken, and the words seared my soul though I understood little of it at the time. I felt I was on the cusp, the crest of a moral tide, a passion that flowed out of the deep—or from the bowels of the lodge. As if something had been said that had to be spoken in parting.

It ceased as quickly as it had begun, slight murmurings fading ahead. And the quiet murmur of the stream and the steady tread of the woman resumed.

Duane squeezed my arm once and turned. We never talked about it again because I do not think we could have described what it meant or how it had made us feel.

We walked on until a huff of cool breeze brought me back to my senses and caused me to realize the scent of the air had changed once more from dank stone to a mossy freshness. I rubbed my eyes. Like peering through green glass, the faintest emerald light played in my vision. Further ahead, I began to make out the vague outline of Duane and the woman. Emerging from darkness, the walls of the cave arched glossy and damp, taller and wider than when we entered at the fallen stones. I was able to look down and see my way beside the stream. When I looked up I could make out the dark eyes of the infant pensively watching, a crooked smile quirked into her cheek.

"Hey, little lady," Duane said, touching her cheek. She smiled and rocked her head playfully.

Our surroundings brightened in stages until we walked from the cave into a twisting, narrow ravine, like the limestone ravines near the old quarry. But the quarry would have been at least twenty miles from where we had pulled our boat onto the beach. Another breeze fluttered tiny ferns like feathers to the top of the walls. The sides of the gorge were tall as a house up to where a ribbon of deep blue sky unfurled overhead.

"Mum, mum, mum," the child chattered again, watching us. The mother replied something pleasant and reassuring, and the child babbled a response.

Snow traced the gray and green contours along the path and dusted the rock shelves jutting from the wall. Though still not comprehending how we could have emerged in winter, we welcomed our warm leather clothing and soft moccasins.

The creek had grown wide. On three polished steppingstones, we followed the woman across the stream and followed a pathway angling upward cut into the side of the ravine.

At the top we emerged into the tawny light of a setting sun. Like the underwater world, everything was bathed golden. With his eyes closed and face turned upward, Duane smiled, took a deep breath and savored the sun. The air smelled—tasted—fresh: as though we had not breathed real air in months.

The woman led on, keeping the edge of the chasm on our right. The child never took her eyes off us.

Soon the woman stopped. She was looking ahead while perched at the edge of a tall cliff, the baby on her back, the sky open in front of her. The ravine we had been walking beside had abruptly ended, cutting a V against the sky.

We stepped beside her and were left speechless.

Where the ravine ended, a waterfall dropped away, glistening and singing as it fell to the bottom of a massive crater that yawned a mile or two across with walls taller than a high-rise, and a floor far below cloaked in haze. Fiborn Quarry would have been a dimple compared to what lay before us. Spread across the bottom of the crater was an enchanted world.

Connected by a river, tiny lakes hemmed the floor of the canyon like a shimmering necklace. Smoke curled from several villages nestled amid towering white pine, pointed balsam, and graceful birch. Children played, men cast nets, and women huddled over their work. Deer scampered through forests where smooth hummocks were outlined by brushstrokes of delicate snow. Across from us, two eagles playfully circled above the valley, twisting and diving an aerial waltz.

"There are many rooms..." Duane whispered to himself.

The woman adjusted the cradle strap over her head and walked along the rim to a crevasse that folded into the wall of the crater, leading downward. We followed, still gawking at the panorama.

Before stepping into the cleft, she stopped and turned to look at us, her brow knit in determination. *No.* Her hands were spread, palms toward us, crisscrossing in the air. *Stop.*

Duane was walking ahead of me. He stepped toward her, wanting to follow, but she blocked the way. In her tongue she spoke emphatically to him, using her hands and shaking her head. While she talked she swept her hand across the crater, pointed at the sky, and nodded in the direction of the cave. I stood back and understood nothing she said, but Duane was listening, nodding his head, and shrugging his shoulders. I had never heard him speak more than a few Ojibwe words.

She made a triangle with her thumbs and index fingers, then swept a hand north from the setting sun. She pressed a finger to Duane's chest, pursed her lips, then abruptly turned. The wide-eyed baby wrapped on the cradle board showed us a tight smile as they descended away from us.

"What are we supposed to do?" I asked.

"She was speaking Ojibwe. It was a little different, but I could understand her." He seemed confused and a little dejected.

"Different?" I asked.

"Yeah, Pops knows some of the language and would say a few words or make jokes. We had a language class in school, but I didn't learn that much. I don't know how..." He scratched his head and smiled sadly.

"What did you understand?"

He pointed at the crater bustling with life. "Um...I don't know, but she used words that I think meant that this is *their* home, *their* village. But it was more like their wigwam or lodge." He scrunched his face, confused. "But it is not *our* place. Not our wigwam. We can't go there."

"Where do we go? Did she say anything that you could understand?"

"North. That triangle shape she made. *Big* triangle. We go north." He looked baffled. "It was weird. She seemed to say it was a way *out*, or a way *home*. I really didn't understand what she meant."

"We have nothing else," I said. "There's no choice. If we keep going north, the setting sun on our left, the rising sun on our right, we must come to a highway or eventually the lake. Where else can we go?" I shivered. "Not back in that cave!"

I expected him to be frightened, but he seemed older again—and stronger. He shrugged. "Right. We have nothing else." He smiled as if to himself, looking back as the round face of the infant disappeared around a corner. "And I trust her."

We gazed across the crater mesmerized. The eagles spiraled downward, spreading their broad wings and tracked a landing on a strand of beach far below.

It came to me. "That's crazy. I think I know what the triangle is," I said.

16

IMAGINATION AND DREAMS

ALL AROUND THE RIM of the crater, a towering forest stood highlighted in slanting rays. The tops of the great white pine were lit green-gold, blending to silver down to dark gray trunks where dim pathways lined with cedar led away from the crater into an ancient forest. Spicey pine scents enfolded us, and the ambient fluting of birds echoed off giant columns.

I thought I knew what the big triangle was about, but first I needed to catch up with Duane. He had trotted off as I was about to get around to telling him all the strange things Miss Jenny had told me. With his endless imagination, we'd had some crazy adventures together, and pretended extraordinary feats, but I was not sure he'd be able to handle what Miss Jenny had told me about the rooms and the planes of time. I had waited to tell him, not certain if he would get frightened or if he would think I was nuts.

While were walking among the floors of the lodge and through the dark cave, I had time to think about what Miss Jenny had told me. So absorbed by herself anything she said was probably unreliable. But some of the things she said were beginning to make sense. No, I would not say they were actually making sense because they were not—could not. But they were beginning to make sense, and I thought I could try to share what she said with Duane and see what he thought. I doubted that it would comfort him, but he often surprised me. And what she said would seem no more fantastic than what we'd already experienced.

Duane circled back to where I sat on a log, and I tried to get his attention. I patted the moss for him to sit.

Not knowing where to start, I scratched my head and took a big breath. "I want to talk about something."

Duane looked at me sideways. "If ya can't spill the beans then you'll eventually smell the gas."

"What?" I asked.

"I think your grandma used to say that."

"Um, no. I don't remember her ever saying that one."

"Or maybe it was *my* grandma." He flapped his hand. "Anyway, you wanted to say something."

I shook my head momentarily, concerned that he would not be able to pay attention to what I had to say.

I turned his way, my bent knee on the log. "Where do you think we are?" I asked.

He leaned forward, folded his hands between his knees, resting his elbows on his lap. "I don't know," he whispered. He looked down, shaking his head.

"Do you—?" I began.

"I'm trying not to think about it. Are we dreaming? Are we in the real world?" He asked with sad eyes.

I had no idea where to begin. Nothing made sense to me, so how could I make it sensible to him?

"Remember when we would play the Indian wars? We made up worlds and it was just like we were in those worlds when we played. At least I know that *you* were lost in those worlds." I nudged him. "It was as though we had gone back in time. I was the Iroquois, and you were the Ojibwe—or Potawatomi, and we were making up real battle scenes. Our spears and arrows were real to us. It was almost like time travel."

"So, we're making this up? I don't get it. It's a dream, then?"

"No," I said, waving my hand. *Maybe I should just give up.*

"I get it." He continued, "But I'm trying not to think about it. I guess I am *pretending to imagine* that this is real. That's how I've been dealing with it since we found our boat parked on the beach again. We knew we might not be in our world anymore. I'm watching. I think that's the only way I can figure this out until my mom, or your parents find us—wherever we are."

I should have known that would be the way he would figure this out, but he still needed to know more. I told him what Miss Jenny had said about the parallel planes of time, the different rooms in a mansion. I explained how, without knowing, we may have crossed over into someplace...*other*.

His brows were knit listening carefully, trying to understand until finally he smiled and interrupted. "Wow. That's so cool. We're like time travelers!"

"Uh, yeah. I guess." That would have to do for now. I was satisfied that he had found a way to put the insanity into perspective. But I had more to talk about.

"You said that the woman pointed north toward a big triangle."

"Yeah. I am sure that her words were big—or great—triangle." He touched his thumbs and index fingers together to make a triangle the way the woman had. "And she pointed that way." He pointed behind us into the great forest.

"Did you ever see the big triangle in the woods?" I asked.

He shook his head, frowning in confusion—or doubt.

"Between Soldier Lake and Raco is the Raco Army Airfield left over from World War II. My mom and dad took us out there one time when we were camped at Soldier Lake. It's huge. Dad said it was supposed to be a staging area to defend the Sault Locks and later held antiballistic rockets that could reach from the Atlantic to the Pacific. Some of these rockets could carry nuclear warheads," I said.

"Cool," he said, peeling bits of moss off the log.

"The airstrips are shaped into a triangle one mile on each side and each strip is wide as a football field. One time we drove back there and got kicked out by the Forestry Service. It is the only big triangle north of the Fiborn Quarry. Even though I know it's ridiculous to believe we're near the quarry." I scratched my head. "I can't say for sure, but I don't know what other *big triangle* she could mean."

He cornered his mouth into his cheek, still doubting me. "C'mon. I do not believe that woman was talking about an air strip."

"No," I said. "But nothing else makes sense here. Like I told you: the planes of time, layer upon layer." I held my hand flat and rubbed my palms together. "Maybe that big landing strip was something else in the past—or future. Do you have a better idea?" I bumped my knee into his thigh. "Play along, kid."

He chuckled. Standing, he brushed off his pants. "Okay. You win. Let's find the great triangle." He pointed into the forest. "Wéch bok—north!" Spoken like a scout.

17

— • —

NORTH INTO FOREST

WITH COLUMNS SOARING THE canopy closed above us like a cathedral. Blades of slanting sun sliced deeply into the darkness of the forest carving stark shadows that danced among the trees.

Amid the incense of pine and damp forest the warble of birdsong far aloft echoed like a canyon. I led along a path that rolled over mossy mounds and brown and yellow evergreen needles. In moccasins, our cautious footsteps were silent.

The weather changed on a whim. In the forest it felt warm as spring, the snow gone. And it seemed strangely familiar; a place we had been before. I could only look at Duane with my brows raised while he made the same expression to me: *Here we go again.*

"Do you think we're almost..." Duane began to say.

I only shook my head. We had been disappointed too often to get our hopes up.

On our right, a soft slope tilted down to a narrow stream. We wanted to believe we were still in a world, or a plane of existence, where streams became rivers and flowed to Lake Superior—eventually.

We followed for a long way as the stream grew wider, lined with deep moss that spread up the banks quilting a shallow ravine. The sun should have set by now, but in yellow light it lingered. The trunks of the massive pines arched away from the edge of the stream until their crown was lost in a lowering haze. We were soon wading through ferns that came to our waist as the brook became wide as a pond, clear and placid. Fish that were gold and silver as coins broke the surface and disappeared into blue-black depths. Like a bow across a cello, we were startled by the *th-rump!* of a bullfrog.

Lacey vines trailed from high above where melodies from hidden birds unfamiliar and exotic showered down. Lily pads dotted the surface of the pond. The air continued to warm, grew more humid, as a thin fog snaked among the tree trunks.

Now we knew we had been here before.

Duane stopped, raising his palm to pause me. Amid the cacophony of forest sounds, we heard the chatter of children far ahead on the other side of the stream. The ferns were taller on that side, making it hard to see the riverbank.

We climbed the bowed trunk of a white pine and crouched on the low branches. Duane gripped my arm when we saw the ferns sway and heard the chatter grow closer. Three figures emerged along a trail on the opposite side of the pond.

"No. Impossible." He looked at me wide-eyed and whispered. Since we had left the edge of the crater and entered the great forest, he had not been frightened. Pitching pinecones and skipping ahead, he was like the playful kid I always knew. But I could tell he was on the verge of panic again. He leaned out and was in a better position to see than I was. I gripped his arm to steady him.

"Impossible," he said again. "Look." He pointed.

Balancing on the tree I tried to see around him, but I only saw three children walking along the edge of the pond.

"That's us!" he said.

I did not understand. I shook my head and leaned further to get a better view. Three children tramped along not a hundred feet away on the other side of the pond. They looked much younger than Duane and me—mere children. But I knew unmistakably I was looking at Duane, Aaida, and the taller kid with the dusky blond hair was...me.

But when? How? We balanced on the branch. I looked at him, he looked at me, and we looked back at the three children. Perched in the tree, Duane and I seemed so much older now. I had noticed Duane looking older, but I had brushed it off as the stress and weirdness of everything we had been experiencing. How had I not realized we had changed so much? Or was this just another bizarre spectacle: some kind of mirror image, time warp, or who knows what? Nothing else made sense in the days, months—years? —since we had been swept away on the rowboat. It seemed like only a day or two.

No. The children looked the way I had remembered on that day at Kwak's Korners. But I realized as we balanced there in the tree, Duane looked as though he could be my age, now. How old did that make me?

"Hey!" Duane suddenly called out. "Hey you guys, wait up."

"No, we don't know what this is. Stop." I reached for his arm, but he had already jumped over onto the next tree and hopped again into a cedar. Waving his arm, he tried to get their attention.

He flapped his arms wildly and jumped up and down on the branch.

While we were in the branches the bridge had been hidden from our line of sight. Shifting to peer around the cedar we discovered we were near the ornate wooden structure that spanned the stream. It arched over the still water, carved with strange inscriptions, twisting dragons, and bizarre masks.

As we pushed through the branches and swung into the trees, Duane continued to yell. The children—we! —looked around frantically. They couldn't see us and were frightened by Duane's shouting, just as we had been at the weird sounds when we were in the forest with Aaida.

Soon sounds echoed back at us. But it sounded like the dreadful cackle of the half human creatures, when they had leapt through the canopy of branches. We could not see them, but we feared the creatures would cross to our side of the bridge.

We panicked in confusion.

We shimmied down the tree and jumped from a low branch. Duane dashed up to the bridge desperately, but the group of three had already fled far down the stream.

"Duane. No, you can't. You don't know," I called.

A flash of lightning split the gloomy darkness of the forest followed instantly by a detonation of thunder. Seen through the forest on the other side of the stream, blackness roiled and covered the sky while our side of the stream was still washed in amber sunlight. Then another flash of lightning hit further away.

I had usually heard thunder only while safely sheltered, never in an open forest. The sound was like the full-throated cry of God across the canopy of sky. The blasting drums of the sky were like sound formed into great dark shapes and sharp contours.

Soon the blackness was spreading to our side of the river, and we searched frantically for cover. The banks under the bridge were built of straight stone walls to the water: no place to hide there. With lightning strikes close by, every tall tree seemed to us a lightning rod. Rain dropped abruptly like a roaring gray wash.

Running wildly, we were soaked and cold in seconds.

"There!" Duane pointed.

A great tree stood outlined like a black tower in the downpour. Three narrow amber lights shimmered eerily from its base. Duane was already halfway there.

"Duane. Duane, wait," I pleaded. How could we trust anything anymore?

"It's the cabin in the woods. I didn't believe it," he shouted over his shoulder.

I didn't know what he was talking about, but another flash and concussive blast and I was right behind him.

18

— · —

CABIN IN THE WOODS

WE LOST SIGHT OF the great tree and the eerie lights momentarily as the flooded pathway circled around a thick grove of cedars. Our moccasins splashed as we made our way quickly around the grove until we could see the tree again and I soon realized the lights were not part of the tree but were set within a low structure beside it.

Through the rain a cabin emerged, built of large logs laid above a chest-high stone foundation. A shower of rainwater was cascading from the broad eaves. At the front, two rounded amber windows were set deep in the logs with a door with patterned glass at the center.

A vaulted cove formed the entryway, shielding the door from rain. Duane darted up the two stone steps, knocked twice, and before I could grab his shoulder, he had opened the door.

"She said it would be empty." He looked hopeful.

In the open doorway, he stood gawking. I eased behind him and reached for his arm to pull him back. "Who said...?" But he stepped away from me, further inside. The scents that escaped through the door disarmed my caution.

I followed.

Fire crackled in a stone hearth, where a round kettle suspended by a cast iron crane steamed and bubbled. I had not thought of eating since we had drifted ashore near the lodge. Duane usually ate anything in sight and even stern Grandma Shirley could laugh at how he would shamelessly pack away food whenever he was around. Now we were both overcome by a ravishing hunger.

The rain pattered on the roof like a stampede of squirrels. A warm aroma drifted from large beeswax candles that shimmered on the mantel, and another sat on the heavy wooden table at the center of the room. The table was set around with four chairs carved with twining vines and snakes. As we stepped toward the table, Duane edged near one of the chairs to admire the carving of a large tree frog set with big red eyes, its back painted in a flourish of gaudy colors.

"Yikes!" he shouted when it warbled, jumped onto the table, hopped to the floor, scuttled across the polished wooden floor, and behind a bookshelf.

The low firelight reflected off the glossy finish of the logs that formed the walls, row upon row hung with hanks of herbs and woven fibers. Next to the door hung a tomahawk. The chiseled stone head of the ancient weapon was secured with leather straps that bound the split end of the long handle. It was not hanging there as a decoration, but scratches and stains on the handle and leather made it clear that it was well-used. Duane hefted it, gave it a couple of swipes—one aimed at me—laughed, and hung it up again.

Drapes the color of golden rod hung beside the windows and the glass in the door. Above a copper basin and wooden water pump, a neat cupboard was stacked with heavy white porcelain cups and dishes. Next to the copper basin on a thick cutting board was a plump loaf of brown bread; a slice lay flecked with grain. Off to the side, a deep pie made of some kind of red fruit and crisscrossed with ribbons of crust sat on a pine counter under a carved cabinet.

For a couple of kids, though lost and hungry, the cabin begged exploration. I stepped to the middle of the far wall near the fireplace. A deep stuffed chair sat at an angle facing the fire and covers on the back and arms of the chair were adorned with twining patterns of beads and porcupine quills. A pudgy footstool sat on a braided rug that lay frayed and thick. On a corner of the rug, near the fire, rested a well-worn pair of beaded moccasins. Against the wall on the left of the big chair stood a wide bed with twisting posts and a carved headboard. A blanket embroidered with more than a dozen squares of woodland and Native scenes lay on top the bed.

Duane had picked up a small sage smudge that burned on the mantel. He waved the smoke into his face and smiled. "My Pops liked to keep a smudge on the mantel when it stormed," he said.

He set the smudge back in its tray, walked over to the cupboard, took a dish, and slapped a slice of bread on it. Then he strode over to the bubbling pot of stew as if he lived there.

"Lentil stew." He got down on one knee and ladled it onto his plate. "Wow. Tomatoes, onions, and spiced just like a grandma would make." He poked at his plate. "And I bet that's venison."

"This is not a good idea. We have to be careful," I said.

"It's okay. I know about this place," he said.

"Do you mind sharing your wisdom? You never said anything about a cabin in the woods," I said.

"Remember, I was not with you the whole time we were in that lodge," he said. "After I left the lobby, you wandered off for a long time, and then I was trying to get you to see me. She told me that Great Grandma lived in a cabin in the woods and when we found it, we would be safe. We would find our way home."

"*Who* told you?" I asked. "And I was not the one who wandered off."

"I don't think splitting hairs at a time like this will be in anyone's best interest," he said with a smirk.

When he parroted adults, I never knew whether to laugh or punch him.

"Aaida. She was with me before we saw her in the hallway." He smiled innocently. "She sure knows her way around." He rustled around near the cutting board until he found a wooden spoon.

"This is really dangerous. We know nothing about this place," I said. "How come you didn't tell me about this before?"

"I don't know. Would it have mattered?" he said. "And that's right. We know nothing. And I'm fine with that. Ooo, that's hot." He followed the stew with a bite of the bread and continued talking while munching. "Some things I would rather not know. Besides, we have no choice. We roll with it. I'm hungry. What's the worst that can happen? We end up in a rowboat on the lake, or in an endless lodge chased by sasquatch or whatever?"

His logic was always hard to argue with.

"When is she coming back?" I asked. "Your great grandmother or whoever?"

He only shrugged, blew on the stew, spooned it onto the bread, and ate. He took a cup from the shelf and filled it at the pump and drank. "Ah. Cold and delicious."

I shook my head as I watched him.

Finally, I could not wait to eat any longer. We did not know where we were or where we were going. What ever happened from our eating poisoned food would happen to both of us.

I dished up, sank back into the big chair arranging a faded blue pillow behind my head. Next to my feet, I set a cup of water on the footstool. In a few gulps, I had bolted the stew and bread and got up for more.

The warmth and the enchanting scents enfolded us.

Duane crawled up on the bed, pulled the heavy blanket over him, rubbed his nose, and lay on his side watching me. I sank deeper in the chair, staring into the fire.

"But I don't want to stay here. I want to go home," he said.

I felt the same way. This place would not bring us closer to what we needed to find.

"We will stay the night and leave in the morning," I said. "Maybe she will come back."

He suppressed a burp. "I don't think she will." His voice was slight, as though to himself.

"Why not? I thought she was your great grandmother."

"Yeah. This is how I would imagine my lost great grandmother would live." He continued to stare at me.

"What do you mean?"

"No. I believe this is where she lives. It's just that..." He held out a piece of parchment.

"What is it?" I asked.

"Read it."

I stretched from the chair to take the note and leaned toward the fire to read the perfectly written note:

To my beloved who follow. I have crossed the bridge. Beyond the Delirium Wilderness is home. I wait for you there.

"Why didn't you show this to me?" I said.

"I found it. I thought it was for me. I had to think about it."

"Why?"

He pulled the quilt up to his chin and looked at me thoughtfully. "I don't know. I thought she meant her family was her *beloved*. That's how Pops or my mom would say it, I guess."

The cabin felt suddenly very lonely.

The windows were like black sockets. I slid out of the big chair, and without gazing out the dark glass, I swiped the curtains closed. There was not a bolt on the door, so I dragged one of the wooden chairs and braced it under the latch. The interior of the cabin still felt warm and protected. But in this world, I could not be too careful.

Looking around cautiously, I stepped back to the big chair, the broad floorboards softly creaking. I heard Duane's deep, regular breathing. The rain had stopped and big drops from the trees dappled the roof. I stared into the fire. Like at the lodge, the fire continued to burn bright and unfaltering without being tended. The night was stoked for visions.

19

A Vision in Embers

TONGUES OF FIRE ARCHED and wavered like tall grasses aflame. Like seething hillsides, a glittering red blanket of coals spread over the logs. The embers writhed like bodies brawling, arms and legs flailing, battling until all bones were broken. Limbs were bloodied where fractured femurs jutted, and shards of arm bones protruded. Yet they struggled on, thrusting their twisted extremities, the flames whispering angry curses.

Sticks lay in the fire like broken and bloodied appendages stacked in the fire. I knew these were *my* broken, bloodied limbs. A burning log settled in a hail of sparks, I gasped, and the entire scene was swept away.

The fire settled to blue green with flecks of yellow in the embers like sunlight on cedar boughs. I drifted deep in thought. A scent like deep, damp, and dying forest infused the room. I stared deeper into the fire until I imagined the lower branches of trees bare, sharp and ragged. A white figure wavered and dodged through the branches emerging from darkness to gray light at the edges of visibility. A ghost? An evil wraith of the forest? One of the hideous ape beasts?

A woman pushed aside the prickly, dead cedar branches and

stepped into a marshy clearing.

Rose Delight White Bird: the White Doe.

Her long braids were twined with beads and leather. She was somewhere she'd never been before. She frowned while at the same time smiling in wonder, her brow knit with curiosity. She wore a long white buckskin shirt with fringes down the sleeves, a yoke over her shoulders patterned with shells and beads and one broad, beaded sash that crossed her chest and another sash sinching the shirt around her waist. Buckskin leggings suited for a warrior were fitted with long tassels down the sides and strung through silver grommets. A ribbon circled each calf above decorated white moccasins that puckered along the top seam.

The vision began to fade as another woman, with long dark hair, dressed in a white robe, came to meet her.

I sat up in the chair, but the vision had already faded.

20

LEAVING

I HAD FALLEN BACK to sleep a long while and was startled awake. The interior of the cabin had not changed: sprawled on the bed, Duane's breathing was raspy and rhythmic. But that was not what had awakened me. There was something outside. It seemed to be a small animal scratching at the foundation of the cabin, moving a few paces and clawing again: a raccoon or squirrel, though other than birds, we had seen no forest creatures. As my head cleared I thought about where I was and that what was outside could be anything.

My concern was justified.

There was a huff as if from the snout of a large animal. I imagined a wild pig with its hideous snot-nosed muzzle of snaggled teeth and its beady eyes. But in this realm, lost in time and place, it could be any dreadful mutant or—

A coarse bawl from a mouth more human than animal. "Hoo, hoo. Ha!" Then more of the snuffling and scratching along the walls of the cabin as it tried to gain entry.

There were sharp raps on the windows, the door rattled, and I knew there was more than one creature out there.

One long, lupine howl and Duane awoke. "What is that? Make it stop!"

He sat up, his head thrashing side to side. "Where are—"

There came a cackle outside the window that sounded like laughter, then a whoosh and thump as a creature leapt from the ground and landed on the roof. Duane's eyes tracked upward. We heard pattering across the roof and back again, and grunts carried down the chimney. I was relieved as the fire continued to burn untended in the hearth.

There was clawing at a corner of the ceiling followed by the loud cracking of splitting wood as shakes were being pried and broken. Excited chatter passed between the beasts from the roof to the ground.

"It's going to get in," Duane hissed, frantic.

Looking to the ceiling, I held a finger to my lips. I looked toward the bread board where the large knife lay.

"The tomahawk," Duane hissed while he sat on the edge of the bed about to jump.

A hairy hand with clawed fingernails crashed through the side window and flailed while reaching close to the knife on the board.

Duane sprang from the bed, swept the knife off the board, and with a clean thrust pinned the paw to the board. A bloodcurdling wail rattled the cabin. The creature tried to withdraw its arm through the window, but the hand was nailed to the board. More screams shattered the stillness of the forest as the board slammed back and forth and the creature tried to free itself.

Duane grabbed the knife handle, the board fell away with a crash, and the scrabbling arm snaked out the shattered window.

With the sound of splitting wood, a sliver of light appeared at a corner of the ceiling. Huffing and grunting, the animal had nearly pried loose one of the roof boards.

Duane and I stood back-to-back in the middle of the room. Harsh cries from the injured beast shook the cabin as the excited efforts of the creatures intensified.

I was about to sprint to swipe the tomahawk off the wall when suddenly the windows were lit with a bright flash, pure white and sizzling. I thought for an instant that the storm and lightning had returned. But there was no thunder, only the startled screeching of the beast intruders.

We could hear as the one on the roof rolled off and hit the ground with a thud. There was another flash, and more howls of torment. But soon whimpering and the rumble of heavy feet were heard receding into the forest.

Then it was silent.

For a long while Duane and I looked at each other, up to the ceiling, around the room, and at the door and windows. Duane still held the knife. He whispered, "What should we do?"

I held a finger to my lips and shook my head. We scanned the room, looking at the damage, and I moved to stand near the hearth and Duane leaned against the bed.

A gentle knocking came at the door, a pause, then three more knocks.

Duane looked at me wide-eyed. Before I could speak, Duane, with the knife cocked over his shoulder ready to stab, sprinted across the room, and was moving the chair I had secured under the latch.

"No! Duane, stop. You don't know..."

Ignoring me, he opened the door a crack, then flung it open.

There was a long pause. "Why are you here? And why are you dressed like that?" he said.

He let the knife drop clattering to the floor, folded his arms, stomped back to the bed, and hoisted himself to sit on the edge, pouting. Without looking up, he said, "I don't want you here. You shouldn't be here."

Dee stood in the doorway dressed just as she was in my vision in the flames. She pursed her lips and looked around the cabin until she settled on Duane.

She shrugged. "Well, I missed you, too," she said.

She had not seen me. I wedged to standing and stepped away from the chair. Dee looked at me with blank surprise, as if she had not expected to find me there. "W-what are *you* doing here?" She said to me, then shook away the thought, "I suppose...I guess..." She flapped her hand. "Never mind. Nothing should make sense, I suppose."

She looked at Duane. "I am here to take you home, son. You don't belong here." She looked at me again. "I am not sure either of you do."

Duane folded his arms again and turned away. "I don't want you here. This isn't safe. It's really screwed up. I don't know where we are, and I don't want to lose you again," Duane said. He sniffled and wiped his nose quickly.

"I know the way out of here. And there is help. I can explain everything, but not yet. Not here. We may not have much time and you must go a little further to get home."

"Through that crazy wilderness of delirium? Is that what you mean? I don't want to go through that place," he said. "Do you even realize what we've been through? It will only get worse."

She shuffled beside Duane and rested her hand on his shoulder. "I am here for you and for Gracie. It was the only choice they left me."

Duane kept things bottled up in himself. He had always been that way. Especially back when Dee was going through her difficulties. Now I believed that Duane knew more about where we were than he had been telling me.

Slowly, he reached his hand around her waist, leaned his head against her, and wept softly. She crouched to be eye level with him. He looked up.

"I will be with you as long as I can. You have more within you than you know. You can do everything that needs to be done for yourself and for Gracie."

"I don't want you to be here. Aaida said we're in a place where you can get lost and never return."

"Is that something else Aaida told you when you wandered off in the lodge?" I interrupted.

"The lodge?" Dee asked.

He waved her off and turned to me. "Yeah, when you and I were separated. I already told you." He wiped his eyes. "She said that when someone leaves their home, they may not find their way back."

"No. You misunderstood," Dee said. She sat on the bed next to him and slipped her arm around his shoulder. "I believe you can go back." She looked up at me a while too long while she spoke. "*You* can go back home, Duane."

"What do you know?" I asked flatly.

She paused, stroking her chin. "I can't tell you more now. You won't understand. But first we must go further on. Then home."

"And what about the dead things? Those beasts?" Duane said.

"What do you mean?" she said.

"I don't want you to be here where the dead things can get you," he said. "Didn't you see them outside? It's a good thing the lightning scared them away or they could have grabbed you."

He stared at her for a beat, thinking. "W-wait. The flashes, then the beasts were gone. was that...?" He shook his head and continued. "When Scott and I got separated in the lodge they almost got me, but Aaida saved me. I don't know how she did it, but she was able to stop them while she hid me in one of the rooms."

Dee nodded.

I tried to interrupt to ask him again why he hadn't told me, but he ignored me.

"Horrible, Mom." He drew nearer to her. "They look like animals, all hairy, but their faces are like dead people. They grunt and try to say stuff, but it is all horrible. Like gibberish. With their dead eyes and sagging lips...ugh!"

She hugged him closer. "Don't worry. That is why I am here. I will try to protect you."

She stood, adjusting her shirt. "It is time to leave."

Duane looked around desperately. "Can't we stay here? Great Grandmother lived here. It's safe. We can't go back out there. It's terrible out there."

"Nothing will be accomplished by staying here." She spoke firmly.

"We don't know how long this place will be safe. Things change."

"And things may not be what they seem," I added.

Dee gave me that long look again, narrowed her lips, and nodded. "That is so true."

We had brought nothing, had nothing to carry, nothing to lose, and no options other than to follow. We pulled on our moccasins and opened the door. Resigned, Duane led us out the door.

The last to leave, Dee stepped back and plucked the tomahawk from beside the door, hefted it, and secured it to the sash around her waist.

Concerned, Duane watched her. "Why are you wearing that stuff that you had at the ceremony? That looks weird."

"And nothing else looks weird here?" She smiled and hugged him around the shoulder. I stared. Either she was smaller, or Duane had grown a head taller. I gave up trying to figure it out.

The day had been washed immaculate. Through haze, myriad shafts of sunlight broad as highways streamed from the canopy to spotlight tree trunks and forest floor. Billowy clouds etched with silver, in regal slow motion, barely skimmed the treetops. A fresh breeze meandered, carrying the scents of deep pine needles and sweet smoke from the chimney.

Dee was already ahead, winding along the path to the bridge, her head high, striding confidently. We scampered to catch up.

We caught up to her at the bridge. We gave her the summary of what we had seen the day before; she seemed to understand. "There are mirrors and there are pathways through mirrors that we can't see."

Duane gave me one of his looks: wide eyes, raised eyebrows, the corner of his mouth creasing a dimple in his cheek. He rolled his eyes. I snorted. It felt good to see him like this.

Dee furrowed her brow. "What? Do you think you know more about this world, smart guy?"

He grinned, hugged her shoulder, and walked on. "Just kiddin'," he said.

Dee chuckled. "I like it." She gave him a quick hug. "Now let's get home."

Her gaze toward me betrayed something again, but I could not tell what it was.

21

— • —

OVER THE BRIDGE

DEE STEPPED ONTO THE bridge without hesitation, but Duane waited for a moment, traced the serpentine carvings of the railing, scuffed his feet, and followed. I wavered longer, recalling the hideous voices when we had been on the other side with Aaida. I also recalled the bizarre reflection of three children hiking the stream and the thunder and lightning forcing Duane and me to retreat to the cabin.

This seemed like a place that would be better to avoid.

But Dee and Duane were soon over the bridge looking back at me. I could only shrug and follow.

"Now you're one of us." Duane smiled, tugging on my leather shirt. I'd forgotten that I still wore the clothes that the woman had given us in the cave. Crossing the bridge, the air felt crisp like fall again, and I was glad I had the leather clothing.

The woods on the other side of the bridge changed quickly as we went further in. It was no longer the same as when we had walked there with Aaida. There were no longer the big trees, ferns, or the mossy ravine. It was like walking beside any ordinary rivulet running through any brushy woodland in the north country.

And now it was autumn. We had come to accept weird seasons that changed without warning. Gray weeds displayed seed pods and bursts of white fluff amid the yellow flags of tamarack and the purple banners of tag alder.

The stream made a broad turn and the path followed. Gravel crunched under our moccasins and the trail became wider until we were ambling on a two-track beside a ditch.

"Does this lead to the landing strip, or big triangle or whatever?" I asked.

Dee stopped while Duane walked on ahead. She laid a hand on my arm. "What do you mean, Scotty? How do you know about that?"

Duane had wandered further ahead, picking stones from the path and batting at them with a stick.

Dee was intent as I told her about the woman and child who led us from the cave.

She watched Duane for a while, then started to say something several times, trying to word it correctly. "I don't know, Scotty. I mean, I know what you're talking about. I suppose the woman didn't completely understand either, or maybe it was not a message for both of you. I know so little." She offered her palm toward the path. "Like a path I can only see a little at a time." She looked at me again. "The triangle, maybe we all go through that place eventually, but I just haven't been given enough insight yet. I don't know what to say."

Her eyes were sad as she looked at me too long again until I had to look away, not able to decipher what she knew; not sure if I wanted to know.

"Let's go." She tilted her head.

Brown marsh grasses grew to the edge of the narrow road and green swamp cedars stood in pools of orange needles. The cool day reminded me of a place like this where Dad, my brother Seth, and I would hunt grouse and rabbits. I expected to see Seth's deer stand around the next corner. West of our home on Bound Road, we hunted in woods just like this.

Wait, I said to myself and stopped while they walked ahead.

There was a trail like this that led into the Delirium Wilderness. Of course: like it had been blocked from my mind. How could I have forgotten that? While floating over underwater lost worlds, lost in a strange lodge, and looking down on woodland villages, it did not occur to me. Of course. It was a place I'd been several times: the Delirium Wilderness. How could I have missed that?

I remembered how my dad had driven us down some logging roads, and we had come in from the north. We parked and walked in on a trail exactly like this. It had been too wet and narrow for our truck.

If this was the same, then I remembered where this trail ended. When I walked it with Dad and Seth, it turned into little more than a mucky trail. We were only able to walk about a mile before we came to a beaver pond large as a small lake. I recalled that on higher ground there had been the frame of a rusty car and flatbed truck left over from an old logging camp or sugar bush. A few cement blocks and some cast-iron stove parts marked where there had been tarpaper camp shacks. Beyond the clearing it became wet and swampy, and my dad did not want to try to go further. The Delirium Wilderness would have been impossible for us to walk through, so Dad stopped, and we went back to the clearing where Seth and I poked around the old camp for a while. The old car and truck had sat rotting in deep grass, their interiors gutted, and the floors rusted through.

I ran ahead to catch up to Dee and Duane. He had been talking, telling her all we had seen. Now he was doing a weird little dance while he destroyed the lyrics to "The Sign" mixing them with "Whoomp! (There It Is)" to create his own song. Being with Dee, he was entirely himself again. He even looked like his young self again.

Smiling fondly, Dee watched him, until she laughed and shook her head.

But I still felt unsettled knowing anything could happen here, and everything was always changing.

"I know where we are, now," I piped up, excited that we may be finding our way out of here. Though I did not want to ruin a moment when things seemed almost normal. "I think this leads to the Delirium Wilderness. We will have to go back. It doesn't go through."

Dee slowed to look back at me, then stopped and shook her head. Through a thin smile she said, "I understand why you're concerned, and I know what you are saying. But no. The only way out now is to go through the Delirium Wilderness."

Dancing ahead, Duane was lost in his own world using a stick as a guitar. She looked at him, her smile sad, then faced me. "You and I have more to talk about. I have not told him everything yet. He wouldn't understand. Someone else will have to tell him." She sighed. "But through the Delirium Wilderness is the only way to get out. Further south and deeper into the Wilderness, then we can go east. You will see."

"Ah!" Duane yelped as several grouse flushed near him. He laughed when he realized what they were, then he yelped again when another flushed on the other side.

More birds took off deeper in the woods near a ragged clump of swamp cedar and yellow tamarack. Dee watched the birds breaking for cover, their wings thrumming. Concern etched her features.

Then the forest grew utterly silent. Nothing stirred. Duane stood alone, looking around curiously.

Near the clump where the birds had flown, the tall tamaracks began to shiver all the way to the top, sending showers of yellow needles. The cedars quivered; the agitated rustling growing until it seemed the branches would explode.

And they did.

22

— • —

GHOULS

"R un!" Dee cried. From scrubby cedars burst braying howls cleft by gurgling grunts peppering the thin forest. Duane ran to Dee, but she pushed him away.

"You must run. I'm behind you. This is why I came," she said.

The ghouls had already closed half the distance, their swinging hands ripping tufts of marsh grass; heads lolling and their dead mouths drooling.

I grabbed his sleeve and pulled him behind me, glancing back as Dee took the tomahawk from her sash. With her lips she pointed down the trail for us to flee.

I shouted. "Duane. *Now*! She'll be right behind," I knew Dee possessed something we did not: skills or a resolve that had brought her here to rescue us.

He stumbled into a run behind me. I feared if we ran ahead down the road, out in the open, we would be easy prey, and I thought our only hope to hide was to find somewhere among the spindly trees and low brush. I slashed off the narrow road, through weeds and scrub, looking for cover.

"No!" Dee cried. "Stay on the trail."

But we were already plunging through grass and tag alder toward a swell of higher ground guarded by a snarled hedge of bristling hawthorn. Amid the hawthorn, a clump of cedar loomed black and thick as a wall. Our leather shirts protected our arms as we swiped through needle-sharp branches.

As I pushed Duane ahead toward the black cedar, a blinding flash behind us froze our shadows onto the dense wall of branches ahead. Sizzling blue-white light attended a withering whip-snapping electrical blare.

I turned in time to see another woman, not as tall as Dee.

Aaida had appeared from nowhere and wielded a sword nearly long as she was tall. She wore a garment bright white and silver. Raising her sword, she crouched in front of Dee, who stood with raised tomahawk as the pack of creatures closed.

The first beast tried to pounce, but Aaida's sword swept off its gangly feet with a hiss and crackle as Dee's weapon slashed its throat into a spray of black blood.

We piled into the cedar branches and fell, spiraling into murky darkness.

23

AWAKENING

I AWOKE IN THE Delirium Wilderness; I believed the Native kid was dead. For a moment I could not remember his name—or my name. A blood smear trailed down the round fender of a rusty pickup and ended above his head. He lay twisted, his arm carelessly draped on the running board, his small hand gray and helpless.

Slate clouds roiled overhead, lowering until the pointed teeth of balsam and black spruce pierced the dark canopy. Leaves and debris were lifted by zephyrs from other worlds, and skittered like tiny feet across the clearing, running over the hulk of the old truck, and back into the black forest.

"Duane," I said hoarsely, remembering. I coughed, my head pulsing like the school fire alarm gnawing at my brain. I would not accept that he was dead. "Duane, we have to…" My tongue was too heavy to speak. The clouds pressed near, surrounding us in darkness.

I tried to hold onto consciousness, sensing a looming danger in the swamp nearby. Something lurked darker and more deadly than the storm, watching us, ready to pounce.

From around the scabby tree trunks, I heard guttural cackling. Wavering from the deep huffing of an ape to the high whining of a hyena, a swinish creature mocked, trying to regurgitate words.

I shifted, trying to see Duane clearly. Was he sobbing? The voice imitated a child's cries. Then another of the horrid voices chimed in, mocking as they closed around the clearing, howling and echoing the gibberish of the other.

The darkening skies closed over me, and my consciousness faded again.

In my oblivion, I was looking down from above as a slow-motion nightmare unwound. Two kids on bikes tear onto a highway, too careless in their renewed summer friendship. A honking horn, a screech of tires, and a brilliant flash off a bike mirror leads to a grinding crash: a twisted bicycle and a body—my body! —in a slow, flailing arc to the ditch.

Grandma had warned me a thousand times to be careful on the highway.

24

—·—

A FINAL AWAKENING

"**S**COTTY, WAKE UP."

I felt like I was slowly drifting to the surface in a river of tar.

"Scotty, wake up. It's time to leave."

Radiating warmth and peace I did not recognize the beautiful face that hovered above. I smiled senselessly like a child watching a glimmering bubble. When the illusion burst it was Dee. And she still looked radiant.

Beside her a different face drifted into focus; just as peaceful and lovely and vaguely familiar. Strangeness fell away to reveal someone no longer a child but a woman like Dee. She allowed a slight smile at the corners of her mouth that only enhanced her beauty.

"Aaida?" I whispered.

Dee tugged at my shoulder to help me sit.

Still dazed I swiveled to take in the clearing. An old rusty car was near, but there was no blood and no Duane. I closed my eyes tight, rubbing my head and trying to remember.

"Where is he?" I asked. "What happened? Is he okay?"

Dee crouched on one knee and nodded to where a small boy

sprawled on the grass; a serene smile, his hands folded on his chest.

"Is he...?"

"No, he will be fine. We will all be fine," Dee said. She gave Aaida an assuring grin. Aaida stood and walked to Duane. She lifted him gently, holding him as if he were her own. He looked so small and helpless again. Dee stood, reached to take my hand, and helped me stand.

I stood taller than her now and my voice sounded like Seth's. I held out hands that were also like my brother's. I patted my head, brushed my shoulders, and realized I was no longer the boy who had grown up in another world.

Dee walked to where Aaida held Duane, stroked his head, and kissed him tenderly. "See you soon, my dear son. Be well."

Carrying Duane, Aaida walked effortlessly to the edge of the clearing where two towering white pine framed a dark arch riling and sparkling. Aaida smiled back at us, raised her chin *farewell,* and they disappeared into a darkness that scattered in rainbows like oil on water and spread to gleaming light.

"Where are they going?" I asked.

"Duane is going back," Dee said.

"We should hurry. Follow them." I pointed.

"No, not that way. That pathway has closed for us. It is far too small," she said.

"W-what? Are we...dead? If *this* is heaven..."

Her eyes squinted with a small wincing sympathy. "Do you feel dead, Scotty?"

I shook my head. I could not imagine feeling more alive. I clenched and unclenched my fists, traced the veins on my arms and felt the blood coursing through my body. I had to smile. "No, I am more alive than I could ever imagine."

"Exactly," she said. "But understand we have passed from our former lives, never to return. Never."

"So, we...died?"

Dee tilted her head and lifted a shoulder. "Would you feel better if I said *yes*?"

I looked away, thinking, then shook my head. "Nope."

She pointed toward a pair of balsams that framed a broad path. "Aaida said that would be your path. She is the one—"

"What kind of person is she? Is she dead...or whatever?"

"She is not a person. Well, she is a person, but not like us."

My brow wrinkled, puzzling.

"Aaida is...celestial. Do you know what I mean?"

"An angel?" I said.

"No. Well, yes, I suppose. I don't know. Here everything is so much more." Dee sighed and waved her hand. "You will see. She has much to tell you."

"She's coming back?"

"I think so, or someone like her, to help us go forward from here."

"But where? I want to go home."

"You will go home, but not in the way you are thinking." She laid a hand on my shoulder. "We have a long way, each of us on a different path. You've heard there are many rooms in the mansion. And you have already seen some but not nearly all of them. They are numbered like infinity upon infinity."

I turned away trying to absorb it all, considering each step we'd taken and contemplating the scenery that was changing even while we waited. I was certain the trees were taller; the clouds were no longer low and foreboding but tumbled silver in a clear sky. The air was cool, rich, and delicious to breath. Everywhere, bird song like flutes and whistles swelled.

"Scott, it is time for us to go forward. I go that way." She pointed at another pair of balsam at the other side of the clearing. "I will follow my mother just like you and Duane did."

"Your mother? No. Then the baby in the cradle board was...?"

She laughed and the bright world brightened more. "You are still thinking in the realm of time."

I shook my head. "You really can't go back, can you? I saw you in a dream. You were tricked by a shaman, weren't you?"

"Not a shaman. But yes, it was exactly as designed and at exactly the right time."

"What about Duane? Gracie!"

She bent to pluck a blade of grass, ran the grass across her lips, and shook her head thoughtfully. Sadness fluttered across her eyes and was gone. "Their pain will be great but exceedingly short. I will see them soon and you will get to see your friend again. There are infinite unknowns—and infinite knowing."

She embraced me. "Thank you for being such a good friend to my son and for delivering him safely through."

"I did nothing." I pressed my fingers to my lips, not knowing what to say next.

"You did everything he needed. What more is there? You should not have crossed over together, but your friendship created a bond that was not easily broken."

She braced her hands on her hips, swiveled, and tipped her head toward her gateway. "The triangle lies north. It is laid of broad stone and surrounds a great village. I will go there to learn, then Aaida said that I would return to join my mother again on yet another plane."

We hugged again, quickly. She pointed toward my gateway again and went on her way.

25

FURTHER ON

T HE PAIR OF BALSAM were like great swords reaching upward into clouds that twirled and drifted around the spires like elegant dancers. The black arch between them sparkled as with diamonds—or stars. As I neared, the darkness faded like walking over a clear ice-covered pond which seems black and deep when approaching, but a world of wonder under foot when crossing. What had appeared to be sparkles were pixels of light that penetrated from a scene that lay beyond the gate.

I passed through into a world of blinding white until my vision corrected by degrees.

My path lay east. Of course, it would. My home had been east of the Delirium Wilderness because that's how it had been designed down through ages, across the planes and layers of time and throughout creation. It could be no other way for anyone: everything designed with precision.

I felt a quaking awe on the other side. I was reminded of the shock of walking into a minus 40° night where stars are like lasers, and frigid breath froze into a sparkling haze or slipped into the lungs like razors. I remembered how trees exploded as they froze and thickening ice over black water sent crazy twanging cracks zipping away into darkness.

As I walked farther in I felt my mind expanding: new channels dug, connections wired in place and secured, missing parts were drifting in from every corner of the universe, fixed into place and booted up, broken edges were mended and polished, switches flipped and brilliant lights coming from everywhere. Forgotten bits were retrieved, every image that had been imprinted was being restored, adjusted, and catalogued. I did not have a skull large enough to hold it all. And the process was only beginning.

All my perceptions and recollections merged and became vivid and immediate. I did not have to glance away or scratch my head trying to draw a memory. All was present and accessible.

In winter during my brief lifetime there had been rare days of that perfect snow, usually in February or March when all the long winter lay compressed and preserved into a hip-deep cover. Then, day by day, the strengthening sun would melt a few millimeters on the surface and at night, it would freeze to form a solid crust thick enough to hike—sometimes even ride a bike—anywhere across the fields or through the forest.

On that perfect snow the skiing was amazing. With a few pushes on the edges, it was possible to fly over hills, cut back, and slice down the side of a shallow ravine. A couple of pushes more and skis would weave around trees like a sparrow.

I had stepped into a world like that. In a realm frozen white there was little chill, only brilliant light. Birches dazzled, cedars were a green never seen, and beech trunks were smooth columns of gray porcelain.

Bird songs flinched and twitted interspersed with warbling scales and arpeggios of varying tempos; every note with countless intonations, their ambience reverberating throughout the forest.

Not walking but drifting, moved by a breeze, I traversed the hills and through endless glades and forests among trees like mountains.

I emerged to an expanse larger than existence. I followed a hedge of hawthorn that arced around a hummock. The bare trees were laden with their small red fruits, the end of each thorny branch curling delicately into a crown.

A herd of buffalo, white in the frost, grazed near the end of the hedge, their great breaths huffing like billows of steam. They could have been as large as elephants, but enormity was lost in this land.

The lead bull swung its head, placidly considering me, every hair frosted and shining silver. Then I saw her standing on the other side. She walked to the animal, reached her arm under its chin and stroked its broad face with her other hand. She acknowledged me with a smile and nod that assured me I had arrived.

She gazed into the beast's eyes, then stepped away. The beast shook its massive head, the motes of frost sparking in the air, and resumed grazing.

Aaida held her hand to me. "Welcome." Her countenance was undefinable: a woman and a girl. Her gown was scarlet, like the hawthorn, and a thin golden crown encircled her black hair.

"Am I home?" I asked.

"Does this feel like home?" she said, smiling.

"I have never been anywhere that feels this much like home."

"Well, there you are." She walked to the hawthorn and plucked one of the tiny apples. She held it up. "On your tiny orb, all things die. They must. It is the way of life. Nothing lives unless something dies." She popped the fruit into her mouth.

"I thought you were—"

"You are learning much, but you will not understand this world until you enter a realm much further on than this."

She motioned for me to walk beside her beyond the herd of buffalo and across the expanse. From our vantage, endless hills and valleys flowed away to the east peppered with lakes and forests. Though it was broad daylight, the steel blue sky darkened to a canopy of stars spanning the sky. There was no Big Dipper or Orion here. These were more than stars; their lights wavered and changed. The radiances floated in a subtle slow dance.

She continued. "On the mortal plane there is no life without death. Death is the inseparable partner of life, the nature of life on earth. You pass on, that's what you do. If there is not death, you do not live. Your Grandma Shirley would have never known you if she were not destined to die and leave your place to grow. Like a forest. You pass on, that's what you do. If the ancients had not passed on, there would not have been room for the next. That is true whether it is the swirling life in a pond or your grandma." She smiled to herself and touched her lips as if to take back her words.

"I won't go back?"

"Do you want to go back?" She asked.

I could not answer for a while. I looked around, I pondered this world and the flourishing tangle of my expanding thoughts. "No, I do not. But what about Duane, what about Dee?" I asked.

"You saw me take Duane. He returned to live there until his final passing from there. His sister, Gracie, will need him. Dee has crossed over from that life and will not return. You saw all this. I know you have: Dee with the evil ones who thought they had intervened but were mere assistants. You saw the automobile accident that crushed your body and injured Duane."

I could not respond. My mind whirled and I could not respond. Thinking of my family, I walked beyond her to look to the horizon.

She approached me and her touch was immeasurably gentle as she continued. "There is so much sadness when one gives their life for another. Such bitter grief when a child dies. I know your concern for your family. But I can offer little comfort because it is not possible to understand the meaning of those things on the other side."

I did not reply.

"But there may be a small drop to quench the despair of Dee's children. Though from where we stand, this far in, there is no going back, but Rose Delight White Bird is one of those rare beings who may yet assist her children from afar. We shall see."

"My parents, my brother, my sister, how will they...?"

Her hand swept to the south, directing my attention. "They will be along soon. Maybe not soon in your world. But incredibly soon here. In the *blink of an eye,* as they say."

Amid a clump of spruce trees and birches, there was a low house with cedar siding and smoke curling from a big stone chimney. Hedges encircled small stone barns.

"I know that place," I said.

"Of course, you do. In my father's house are many rooms."

"It's just like Bound Road where I grew up."

She smiled.

"We were either snow bound or glory bound, they always said. How did I get back here? Everything is so different."

"Why do you think you had to go anywhere? The worlds touch. You've always been here. Where would you go? One brick is built upon the one beneath. Walls are built on foundations. The next chapter is built upon the story before it. You will go further in, but you will always be here. It cannot be explained. Not yet."

I stood looking up at the dancing stars, trying to fathom that which was unfathomable. I held between my thumb and finger all the world I had known and all the knowledge I had acquired as a child. Everything here was too large. No one could return from here to their previous life. It would be like a butterfly returning to its cocoon or an adult to the womb.

When I turned, Aaida was gone. The buffalo huffed on the slopes. The air was warming toward spring, and I walked toward Bound Road.

From here I live on in your memories, your healing grief, and I will always whisper to you in your dreams.

The End

ACKNOWLEDGMENTS

This book contained many autobiographical references and I kept it close to the vest and all in the family. As I've noted before, writers are a dime a dozen, but great readers are truly rare. And Sally is the greatest reader. I would not want to write a paragraph without her incisive eye and ready red pen.

Also special thanks to great nephew Gavin Tilberg, though a bit older than Scotty and Duane, he gave me excellent insight. He was one of the few kids to have read *Dead of November*, so he was gracious when I asked him to read an early draft of *Delirium Wilderness*. Thanks to our kids Jonah and Sarah and daughter-in-law Amie for enduring my requests and putting up with how I too often bring the conversation around to writing.

Much thanks to Michaela Bush and Tangled Up in Writing for editing and proofreading.

Michigan's Upper Peninsula will remain my muse, and all those fantastical though very real places like the Delirium Wilderness, Fibron Quarry, Naomikong, and the trilling swamps and remote forests are forever in my dreams.

About the Author

Craig A. Brockman lives in Tecumseh, Michigan with his wife, Sally (muse, mentor, and the most insightful reader in the world). He has also written the award-winning *Dead of November: A Novel of Lake Superior, Curve of the Earth: A Novel of Lazarus* and the middle-grade novel *Marty and the Far Woodchuck.*

For more information go to craigabrockman.com or email craig@craigabrockman.com.